# Of WHAT WAS, NOTHING IS LEFT

## A SUSPENSE-PACKED TALE OF ARKANSAS

2/14/2020

# OF WHAT WAS,
## NOTHING IS LEFT
### A SUSPENSE-PACKED TALE OF ARKANSAS

## BY
## FRED STARR

Thank you to John Oates for his creative contributions.

Special thanks to Cindy Starr, Chris Epting,
Craig Shelburne, and Tracey Yee

Cover Illustration by Shane Miller

Art Direction by McClearen Creative

Photography by McClearen Creative,
iStockphoto and Shutterstock

Reprinted version dedicated to
Grandsons of David Starr...
Carter, Lincoln, and Gabe Sloan

Original dedication from the author:
To Elder Hayes,
Whose Friendship Furnished Inspiration For This Book

*"A grandfather is someone with silver in his hair and gold in his heart."* – Author Unknown

# FOREWORD

Inspiration is truly a phantom. You never know when or even if it will appear. Or how it will present itself. It's like a shadow that can either linger like wood smoke or disappear in the blink of an eye. That's why you always have to be ready. Maybe it's the way a warm wind cuts through the tops of the pines. Or how she smiled at you before allowing her gaze to linger. Perhaps it's a scent. It may even be a story that you read; some long-ago voice filtering down the wisdom of the ages in the form of a book. For those of us who still love the magical feel of paper when we read, a book can provide more than just a spark of inspiration. It can present you with an entire road map that will help steer you toward the art you know you are capable of creating.

That's what happened to me after I read *Of What Was, Nothing Is Left*. It was written by my beloved grandfather, Fred Starr, whom we thought so close to that we called him Dad. It's hard for me to measure just how much this man shaped my mind and soul. He taught me to ride and break the Shetland ponies he raised on his 40 acres on the south edge of Fayetteville, Arkansas. Thanks to him, I learned that you just have to get back on the horse, both literally and metaphorically. He enjoyed taking me for walks in the nearby hills that are now scarred by a busy interstate highway and subdivisions.

It was on one of those many strolls that we came upon an old cemetery where we talked history and destiny. To this day, I'm not sure why. Fate just playing its hand, I suppose.

I was always aware that he was an educator, a state legislator, a newspaper columnist and an occasional novelist. Most of the books he wrote, I was told, were a reflection of the Ozark hills and the people he loved so much. But I never thought of him in the light of "writer" or "creator." To me, he was first and foremost, a buddy; a man who taught me about the outdoors and stubborn little horses. He was an adult who seemed not to judge. As a grandfather myself now, I certainly understand why.

While I grew up believing I knew him fairly well, it wasn't until I finally read *Of What Was, Nothing Is Left* that I really began to know my grandfather as a creative soul. Eloquent, honest and compelling, his storytelling skills were exquisite. Unlike his earlier "folk tale" works, this book was a work of fiction set in rural southwest Arkansas. The sandy soil and piney woods of that region provided the backdrop for a story of tragedy, family dysfunction, and denial. I'd avoided reading anything of his after he passed away. Maybe I just wasn't emotionally ready. Perhaps some latent grief kept me from wading into his words. Regardless, once I read this story, I experienced an awakening. The book was more than just a sweeping tale.

It was my new inspiration.

In it, I found a saga that is both as old as mankind and yet still relevant today. The story speaks to our decisions blinded by passion, our human frailties, and our enduring flaws. From the Garden of Eden to today's headlines, the story resonates now as much as ever. But what could I do as an artist in reaction to it?

I first gave my friend John Oates a copy of the book to read. "I love the story," he told me. "It's rich and fascinating. But what do you want to do with it?" And I told him, "I want to get you and other songwriters together and build a concept album around it. I want other artists to think about the parts that move them and then start writing." Thankfully, John thought that was a strong idea and he and the great Jim Lauderdale got together with myself to kick around a few ideas. I also gave a copy of the book to Irene Kelly (who, wonderfully, said it conjured up "*Wuthering Heights* in the old west"). I gave one to Dana Cooper and to the Wild Ponies, aka Doug and Telisha Williams. I gave a copy to Shelley Rae Korntved, who manages Starr's Guitars (my guitar store) and my friend Wood Newton. This was the dynamic: Find the part of the book that inspires you and react to it with either music or words. The idea was not so much for them to re-tell the story, but to write songs inspired by the places, characters and situations found in the book. It was just that simple. That's how "Beauty and Ruin" was born.

As a writer, this book freed me up incredibly. I tend to live in my own head and write about myself. Now, all of a sudden, I had an entirely new cast of characters to direct my creative energies toward. It was so liberating. Then I would begin to weave my own stories into what I was writing and the book at once became a conduit; a tunnel to another dimension. During the writing and recording process I endured a life-threatening medical situation which I soon translated into the song "Rise up Again." My own personal conflicts were blending with the narrative in the book and I heard from all of the other writers that they experienced similar moments of "line blurring."

In the end, what we are left with is an organic and expressive set of collaborative pieces that reflect a greater whole.

The book is what started the process, but we all finished with our own creative inspirations.

Inspiration is truly a phantom. You never know when or even if it will appear. But for myself and this marvelous group of writers and performers, it appeared many times over through the course of this project which I now, with great pride and satisfaction, present to you.

*David Starr*

OF WHAT WAS, NOTHING IS LEFT

# TABLE OF CONTENTS

# CHAPTER ONE

He is gone now. His cottonfields, once so patiently tended by the negroes, are choked with sassafras and persimmon sprouts and overrun with old field pines through which the winter winds sigh night and day, as if in mourning for those who once toiled and sweated; laughed and cried here.

Around the family burying ground, where so many of his kin have taken up their long sleep, the fence posts are rotten, the palings fallen in decay, and the gate – hanging on rusty hinges – cries like disturbed ghosts with each fresh gust of wind.

Sitting on the rotting steps of the Big House, through which mice scurry, and around whose walls the wind asks questions without answers at the doors and boarded windows, I can hear the clop, clop echoes of the Maude mule coming up the lane, and the Cap'n's voice – not unlike the bellow of a huge bull at mating time – singing a song without words.

I can see the negroes pouring from their cabins back of the Big House like water from a broken jug; the big ones to take the reins of the Maude mule, the little ones to challenge each other over the candy and chewing gum the Cap'n tossed from the huge pockets of his hunting jacket.

Captain Johnson was a legend in the Laurel Creek settlement from the time he came home from the Spanish-American War his chest heavy with medals and wearing the title, Cap'n, he was to be called forever and a day.

In all this strange land of cowbells, rail fences, coon dogs, and old field pines, there had never been a man quite like the Cap'n. At age eighteen, he had taken his foot in his hand and run away from home – something unheard of on Laurel Creek, where young bucks married at an early age, moved into a weaning house built by their sires, started a nest of youngens, and settled down to a life as tasteless as branch water and as unexciting as a bale of hay.

The one thing immutable here was the poverty of the soil. The sandyland took much and gave little except the bare necessities. It seemed to destroy everything precious to the inhabitants except the will to live and the ever-present concern about what was happening and had happened to those about them.

So they worshipped from afar this man who dared to be different. He had been West to the fascinating land of cowboys and Indians. He had spent long days and lonely nights on cattle drives, eating dust in summer and feeling the cutting winds and snows in winter. He had ridden with the courageous and dashing Teddy Roosevelt, in the excitement of war and – whatever else he was – he was a hero in their sight.

The Cap'n came back from the war to his homeland where there was little left to call him. His parents had recently died – one day apart – with complications of measles and pneumonia. They had been buried in a single coffin, in a huge grave in the family burying ground a stone's throw from the front porch of the Big House.

This man had never married, and he was going on nigh forty when I came to know him. Oh, he was handsome enough, with hair black as midnight under a skillet; a broad mouth with thick lips, made – the women said – for kissing.

He had teeth that flashed white when he smiled, which was most of the time. He was a big man; big all over, and carried himself proudly as though royal blood ran in his veins.

The Cap'n lived all alone in the Big House, with its tall fourposter beds, piled high with ticking filled with feathers from the geese that helped the negroes keep the grass from the cottonrows stretching across the 160 acres of land.

Besides the huge, canopied beds, there were rooms of furniture enough to stock an antique shop. All this was carefull tended by Lizzie, the negro woman who did the housework. The Cap'n's bed – where he did not always get home to sleep – was covered with a Star of Bethlehem quilt that his mother had made for his wedding night, and the pillows were covered with spotless shammies on which had been crocheted "God Bless Our Home" and "Christ Is the Head of This House."

I can still see the kitchen whose rough board floor was sand-scored to bone whiteness, and the barrels of flour and sugar in the corner; the hams hanging from the rafters, and the rows on rows of canned goods in glass. I can smell the beans, black-eyed peas, cabbage, turnips and collards; blackberry cobblers, egg custards, and all the varieties of food that were daily heaped upon the home-made table where any and all guests were welcomed. Nobody went away from the Big House hungry, and the host would have been highly insulted had a passer-by at mealtime refused to stop long enough to hitch up a chair to the table and eat his fill.

We came to this sandyland and pineywoods settlement from far off Ohio – another world way yonder to the natives. My father had wanted a farm of his very own, but land in this north country was hard to come by, the price being what it was. When his uncle died and left him an eighty-acre farm in Arkansas, we piled what few worldly goods we possessed into a big covered wagon. With a pair of Percheron mares beside the tongue, we came to claim father's inheritance; strangers in this strange land where few of the inhabitants ever left, and still fewer sojourners ever wandered in with the idea of staying on.

We had hardly divested the wagon of our few household goods and set up housekeeping, when the Cap'n rode up to the gate on his Maude mule, helloed the house and told my father his business. He was in the market for a pair of mares such as ours. We had no earthly use for these huge animals to snake a Georgia stock up and down cottonrows; pissle-tailed mules would do a better job, and a one-horse wagon would serve all our needs, while only our big wagon would serve his. He had a convincing manner and a conniving way about him and his talk made sense. My father didn't want to part with the only thing he had left to be proud of – as badly as we needed money – but the Cap'n dared him to set a price.

And when he did, the man reached into his saddlebags and pulled out a wad of greenback big enough to choke his Maude mule and counted the right amount into my father's hands. This part of the transaction done with, the Cap'n looked at me with those penetrating, pitch-black eyes of his, and said now he needed a swamper; somebody to drive the team. The pay he offered for the service of a strapping, overgrown, fourteen-year-old boy was better than could be hoped for.

So then and there I became part, parcel and slave to this man. He reached down from his perch astride his huge Maude mule and put his heavy hand – like a bear's claw – on my head. With a mellowed dignity, and a voice like Saul bestowing the kingship on little David, he said in his booming way, "Boy, hitch up our team and come on over to the house. I'll be waiting for you."

With that he waved to my father and was gone up the lane, his Maude mule in a kind of running walk; a gait never slow and never fast, but one to take her master over three counties the quickest way there was to get there in those days before a man named Henry Ford was to provide a faster – if not a cheaper – mode of getting from one place to another.

As I watched the man ride away from our place, the 200 pounds of him sitting in the saddle like a king of old on a throne, his broad back straight as a ramrod, I thought about Alexander the Great crying in his cups because – at the age of twenty-six – there were no more worlds to conquer. And I figured that had the Cap'n been there, he would have gone forth at the head of his army and found more worlds in spite of hell and high water.

As I drove across Laurel Creek and headed up the lane to the Big House, and saw him standing on the porch shading his eyes from the evening sun, all at once I was overawed and felt – as badly as I knew my father needed the money for my hire – that I couldn't go through with it.

Today, looking back, I keep repeating to myself the poem about the traveler who came to the forks of the road, took the one less traveled, and always wondered what would have happened had he seen fit to take the other one.

Once inside the Big House, under the spell of the Cap'n, all my doubts vanished like the morning mist over Laurel Creek at the sun's coming-up. It was early spring. The negroes had laid a little fire in the big fireplace to chase the night's chill away.

Supper was a feast of fried ham, streaked gravy, hot biscuits, pear preserves and all the kinds of vegetables a woman could can from a garden, along with plenty of thick butter-milk to wash it all down.

The Cap'n ate with a relish, wiping his mouth at intervals with a snow-white napkin which he tucked into his shirt collar beneath his firm and protruding chin. He kept urging me to have more of this and some of that, until I grew weary from declining and wished for more room to pack away such delectable victuals.

Sitting before the fire that night, with my host in a tall, ladder-backed, hide-bound-bottomed rocker; the glow from the fire lighting up his ruddy features, I was led step by step into the land I was to inhabit for what proved to be more years than I had lived up to then.

The Cap'n was a cattle buyer. He roamed the country astride his Maude mule and dickered with the farmers for any surplus stock they had. My job was to follow with wagon and team and a well-defined map – drawn from memory by the buyer – and pick up said purchases, cart them to Jubilee, the nearest town eight miles away. There the animals were kept until a carload had been accumulated. They were then shipped to Shreveport, sixty miles away by rail, and a week's travel to and from by horse and buggy.

# CHAPTER TWO

The first two years of my stay with the Cap'n passed as years have a habit of doing. They were golden days. I seldom saw my family except on Sunday when I went to turn in my weekly earning over to my father. Sometimes on week days, as I sat on the spring wagon and passed by the field where my brothers and sisters were chopping cotton, hoeing corn or cutting sprouts in the summer's galling heat, I smiled smugly to myself and pitied them, laboring away like peasants while I rode a royal wagon in the service of a king.

For king the Cap'n was to me. No matter how long the day, how dark and stormy the night, I always made it a point to return to the Big House in hopes he would be there. When he wasn't, the rest of the night would be long and I would toss in my big bed in the fireplace room like one with fever.

In winter, when he was home, I lay bug-eyed, my hands folded behind my head, with the firelight making strange figures on the walls, I listened to him talk of Indian raids and cattle drives; of riding against the enemy with Teddy Roosevelt, of the trips to the big city and his strange and fascinating business of buying and selling. In summer, we sat together on the front porch, while I imagined the fireflies to be the lanterns bobbing about the campfires of those long cattle drives and nights spent in army camps.

To hear the Cap'n tell it, no transaction he made in the cattle business brought any profit. When he bought, he paid too much, and when he sold, he didn't get enough. Yet he always had pockets of money that sometimes overflowed into his saddlebags. Every time he came home from the far-off magical city, he brought me a present; new gloves or ties, socks or underwear, shirts and pants. Often there was a bonus in money far beyond the dreams of my father, whose large family's needs seemed to outrun the intake in spite of all we could conjure up in the way of money.

At Saturday night parties, Sunday church and all-day sing-ings, I was surrounded by boys my age who were anxious to hear tales of the Cap'n's exploits in Shreveport, where they said he was known to cut a wide swath. Their meager lives were not crowded with any more excitement than a once-in-a-great-while trip to Jubilee to Saturday afternoon drawings and play parties on Saturday nights. They were starved for adventure such as the Cap'n might be exposed to in that city of sin. They seemed to feel that one in my position – a sojourner in a strange land – could add color to the conver-sation just by the plain facts, or mere hint at what went on where the big man in the Big House was concerned.

Maybe I was selfish, but my talks with the Cap'n were a part of my very being. To repeat any part of them would be sacrilegious. I was old enough to know he wouldn't bother to tell me everything, but when they asked if he ever spoke of going to the red light district, I grew hot and trembling with anger and resentment. I threatened to bash in any dirty mouth that even hinted he might stoop to such.

One night, as I watched the Cap'n get ready for bed and climb under the softness of the covers, I wondered if he ever felt the need for a woman, and why he didn't get married. Before I knew it, I was telling him what the dirty-minded

24

boys had asked and what I threatened to do about their questions.

He raised himself to a half-sitting position with his fine head resting in the cupping of a hand; an elbow for a prop. His eyes burned like the coals of fire in his handsome face as he said fiercely, "Some folks remind me of a feist dog what gets excited and leaves his mark on everything he can lift his leg to. Now when a boy the likes of you, puts men the likes of me on a pedestal, sooner or later he'll find we have feet of clay. So don't you go thinking I'm perfect, because I'm far from it. I've helped hang my share of cattle thieves and broke up a smart deal of furniture in barrooms brawls. When younger, I thought I was a devil with the women – just like most all young bucks imagine themselves to be at one time or another."

He paused, shook his head sadly, and continued, "I'm no saint by any stretch of the imagination. Some things I've done, I'm ashamed of, and some I've bragged about. But whatever I've done, it's no concern of a bunch of boys not yet dry behind the ears. Now you're old enough to know that thing between your legs was put there for something besides carrying off waste water. If you was my son, I'd say to you, 'Keep it in your britches until you get a marriage license in your trunk.' I'm sure your Pa would give you the same advice. Now let's get some sleep. Tomorrow's going to be a hard day."

I just couldn't believe it! I just couldn't! But if the Cap'n said it, that was bound to make it so.

Sometimes the Cap'n would broach the idea I should be in high school, but I knew – and he knew – my folks were having a struggle to keep the wolf of want from giving birth to pups on their doorsteps without losing my income and taking on the added burden of boarding me at Jubilee, while I was at school. Besides, I couldn't think of the time ever coming when I would not be just a boy, pulling the lines over a pair of Percheron mares, getting stared at and envied while I hauled squealing and grunting hogs and lowing cattle to stockpens for the Cap'n. That was far better than anything education could get me.

It was again early spring. The dogwood and redbud were full blown. Birds were mating and nesting. Frogs were drumming in chorus from the low places. Laurel Creek was running bank full, and the field hands were breaking the land to put in another crop.

The Cap'n had never spoken an unkind word to me. But lately I had pulled a boner that I was afraid would cost him plenty and bring down his wrath upon my head.

He had bought a boar. When I went to pick him up, the owner was not at home. I loaded the wrong hog. When I arrived at Jubilee, the stockcar was being loaded. This gentleman hog, with a pedigree long as from here to yonder, was put aboard, taken for a ride and converted into sausage before anybody knew the difference. The Cap'n had offered the owner a fat price for the mistake, but not enough. Now he was being sued.

When I first learned of this, I was horrified. "Why didn't I know better?" I asked, choked with frustration.

"Hell's bells!" stormed the Cap'n, pacing the floor. "What does a boy your age know about fancy hogs? Don't they all look alike? Sure, you know a boar has four legs, two ears, a snout, a couple of eyes, a pair of balls and a tail. But a pedigree! Not many hogs can afford such a new wrinkle."

"But for you to be sued all on account of my blunder!" I cried shame-faced.

"It's none of your fault. Somebody ought to have been there to show you which one and to help load him." Suddenly he stopped his pacing and bellowed, "Bygod, if he wants a fight, we'll give him one. We'll scrap him until hell freezes over. Now don't you go blaming yourself."

At breakfast the next morning, the Cap'n was jolly as a magpie. He laughed and joked with Lizzie who was waiting table. Raking her with a teasing light in his coal-black eyes, he asked, "Lizzie, what would you say if I was to tell you we're about to have a mistress for this big, empty hollow-sounding house?"

"Lawd, Mr. Cap'n," Lizzie exclaimed. "That would be like old times when your Ma was alive. I'd shore cotton to the likes of that!" And I almost choked on a piece of ham I forgot to chew in the excitement.

"Boy," the Cap'd said to me, "hitch Charley to the buggy and meet the two o'clock train at Jubilee. There will be a lady on there who'll answer to the name of Laura Weldon. Fetch her home with you and stop long enough at Preacher Biglow's to tell him to show himself here at seven o'clock sharp tonight."

Surely my astonishment was something to see. I must have looked as Adam did when God told him to get himself out of the Garden of Eden.

"I'd meet her myself, but I've got other things to do." He noticed the expression on my face. "Now, boy, don't you go worrying your head none. Everything's going to be all right."

Sure, everything was going to be all right for him. He wouldn't have to give up his place in the fireplace room and crawl off to himself in a big bed in a cold room, with nobody there to talk to and no more stories about the war and cattle drives. He would have somebody else to talk with about Shreveport, where there was somewhere to go and something to do every night the whole year through.

There would be nobody to care whether I got back off the drive at night, and how wet I got from summer rains, or how cold I got when the north wind sang. Cap'n would have a woman and he wouldn't have time to think or care about me. I might as well quit, go home and make believe I had never left to become the slave of this man.

The negroes curried Charley until his sorrelness shone like new money. The rubber-tired buggy, with the umbrella top – lately bought, and now the mystery of why had been solved – was polished to perfection. As I climbed in and started on this fateful journey, I wondered if the woman who was getting all this attention, was the kind like Cinderella, or if she were more like her sisters. If I hadn't picked up the wrong hog at the wrong time, I could have been home sulking and the Cap'n could be running his own chores.

The train, which could have easily been wrecked and delayed the misery a few hours, was right on time. It came hooting into the station with each clang of the bell striking my heart like a stone. The conductor handed down a big-bosomed, stringy-haired painted woman who must have lately been somebody's mistress. I hoped she wasn't Laura Weldon. I crossed my fingers and shut my eyes for a minute. When I looked again, I saw this picture framed by the door-facing of the day coach. She wasn't large and she wasn't small, but just the right size. I couldn't see her face for her veil, but as the porter helped her down and lowered her suitcase to the platform, she lifted her face covering, looked directly at me and smiled.

Then she tripped toward me, and I smelled the fragrance of lilac, honeysuckle and jasmine all rolled into one. Although I was not a man grown, I felt a catch in my throat and a strange emotion of elation that her presence was to arouse in me throughout the long years I was to know her.

"I just know you are Frank!" she exclaimed. Her voice started the ringing of bells in my ears. I must have brightened as if a candle had suddenly been lighted in my insides. Then she kissed me. I had to steady myself to keep my balance. The hate I had for her since breakfast went out of me like the coldness of winter going out of the ground when sunshine falls on the sandyland like a benediction, and warm south winds fan new life into the cold earth.

All the miles from the station she chatted incessantly. She told how the Cap'n had said so many nice things about me; how glad she was to get away from the crowded city to a place where she could breathe again and stretch and look up and see the clouds float lazily by in the daytime, and where the stars peep out one my one at night and then by dozens and hundreds, like flowers in a spring meadow.

She could hardly wait to see the Big House and meet all the Cap'n's friends. I didn't tell her he had few close friends, and that the Big House might have a tendency to smother her at night when the Cap'n didn't come home. I didn't tell her how lonesome she would get all the days he would be too busy losing money to think about anything else – even a lovely lady such as she must be.

Even though I liked her very much, and could see – as young as I was – that she was all woman, and how lucky the Cap'n was, I couldn't help but feel that a very vital part of my life was at an end, and I didn't like what I saw. With

her around, I reasoned, I'd never again see the frozen hills
the Cap'n had ridden over as a cowboy in search of cattle,
and the blinding rocks of the sun-bleached desert's heat over
which the herd wandered north to market.

# CHAPTER THREE

They were married that night in the little-used parlor; the ceremony lasted longer than the Cap'n had spent there the two years since I had come to live with him. The bride bubbled over with the excitement of it all. I felt her laughter, constant talk and gaiety were but a cover-up for a buried dream she once had of a big church wedding, with music, a great reception, important people everywhere, and not just a preacher, a shy youngster and a few wall-eyed negroes for an audience.

If the Cap'n – loud, boisterous and bold – was a legend in the Laurel Creek community, Laura became a symbol of all that was gracious and charming. The women of the settlement were invited to a party the very first week after the wedding. The Cap'n took his new bride to town one day and dispatched me the next to haul home a grand piano. There was music and dancing feet of the young folks they played Skip-to-my-Lou and Pig-in-the-Parlor.

Laura tried and failed miserably to make the Cap'n a part of her entertaining. If he learned about her parties in time, he rode his Maude mule to the farthest corner of the county, fleeing from what his wife said was his bounden duty. If he could not escape entirely, he shied away from the guests, excused himself early and went for a walk or hunt with his dog, Music.

He left me to play the part of host on occasions. I did the best I could. Laura often heaped praises on my efforts, at the same time giving out little sighs, wishing the Cap'n would be more sociable. In the same breath, she would attribute his lack of such graces to his barren bachelorhood and natural shyness.

I drove the new Mrs. Johnson in the buggy to every public gathering for miles. We attended all-day singings on Sundays and took with us a trunk of food Laura spent hours preparing the day before. She spread it with the other women at noon. The men were drawn to her by her charm and beauty and her desire to please. The children followed her as if she were Laurel Creek's lady Pied Piper.

With the women things were different. While the men bragged on her chicken pie, egg custards the heavenly cakes and rolls, the women whispered behind her back about how uppity she was. They were of the opinion the food she so proudly and daintily placed on the rudely constructed tables under the trees surrounding the church, was prepared by the negroes. They ventured to guess she couldn't boil water without scorching it.

If Laura noticed their jealousy and overheard their unkind remarks, she never let on. She invited them to the Big House at every excuse. The women came to protect their social standing in the settlement. They also felt a need to look after the menfolks who lost much of their self-consciousness under the spell and hospitality of the hostess of the Big House. She took flowers and food when she visited the sick. Her presence was said to be more effective at times than the medicine prescribed by old Doctor Jordan.

With the Cap'n gone much of the time, I had many long talks with Laura there in the fireplace room where their marriage had been consummated, and where I had spent so many happy hours with her husband. At bedtime she would follow me to my room, turn back the covers as though I was a small child and kiss me goodnight. It was as if she realized things were not as they had been between the Cap'n and me, and she tried desperately to make up for being an intruder. Years later, I was to learn that that was not the reason at all.

After she left, I would lie there, wide-eyed for hours. I tried to pierce the canopy of the huge bed and thought if I could see beyond it, I could glimpse through the glass darkly – that the Good Book speak about – and figure out who two totally different people could be in love and married, and why her presence affected me so.

At times I felt Laura was violently unhappy. She chafed and fretted at the Cap'n's constant absence. Such had little or no effect on the man. Somebody had to make the living, he argued. Many afternoons, she had the negroes hitch Charley to the fancy, rubber-tired buggy. Once with the lines in her hands, she would send the horse racing down the lane, to leave the Big House, where the walls were pressing around her; to seek open country and surcease from her loneliness. She often spoke of her friends yonder in the city. Sometimes I feared to come in from a trip; afraid she would be gone from whence she came, taking with her what sunshine there was left.

She told me over and over about wanting seven children – a magic number she called it – four boys and three girls. She wanted her first born to be just like me. But after six months of her sleeping with the Cap'n, I saw no sign of swelling of her middle, and I doubted if there would ever be a first born, much less others; not while she was married to her present husband.

One day, after I saw the Cap'n go off to market with a load of cattle, I came home to find Laura entertaining a peddler from Bussey. As I drove up the lane, I noticed his horse tied to the oak in the front yard; the big oak she so often said would furnish shade for her children and her children's children. I could hear her tinkling laughter as it floated through the window before I whoa-ed the team. She greeted me with flushed face and introduced the peddler as if he were not selling notions at all, but was a dispenser of the happiness she had come to the Big House to seek and failed to find.

He was a handsome Rudolph Valentino sheik of a man in his late thirties, perhaps. But if you put him up beside the Cap'n, he couldn't hold his elder a light to see how to shuck corn by. Yet there was something about him that was bound to appeal to the woman part of Laura. In his pack he had everything from needles and pins to dress goods, cosmetics and perfume. Maybe visibly he was selling things to please a woman's vanity, but to me he peddled trouble – a bucketful of it in each hand.

I had no way of knowing how long he had been there. Night was coming on and Laura insisted he stay for supper. She left me to entertain him while she tidied up a bit. I was dumbfounded on her return to see she had dressed in her Sunday's best.

Throughout the meal she kept asking this Mr. Vaughn about himself. She laughed too loud at any excuse; her hands fluttered to her hair and face and back again like moths around the kerosene lamp. All the time I could see the Cap'n waving to me from the back of the caboose and hear him saying, "Look after Laura," in the strange tone of voice he used so often of late when he spoke of her.

Her husband had gone to market to get more money to

buy more things to make his bride of six months happy. Now, here she was, blushing, letting her eyes say things they never should say to a stranger, and there was nothing but nothing I could say or do about it. All at once I felt like a traitor to the Cap'n and a stranger to the woman who was the sweetest and most precious no-kin thing to ever come into my life.

Laura wanted some piece goods Henry Vaughn didn't have, but when he left – after holding her hand longer than I thought necessary – he promised to come back tomorrow with just the cut of cloth she desired.

She forgot to come to my room after he left, but sat on the doorsteps and looked up the road the way he had gone. The moon made a halo around her head of hair, golden as fresh-cut wheat straw in the sun. I tossed for a long time before I heard her go to her room. I lay for what seemed hours and listened to the plaintive cry of the whippoorwill from the woods back of the barn, wondered about love, and why so many had to get hurt so much all because of it.

Laura did not come to breakfast the next morning and I was glad. I hurried out to help the field hands in the cotton. I didn't want to see her flutter like a high school girl with her first love, and hear her gay laughter. The night before had told me all I wanted to know.

Did this woman imagine she was in love with this man? I wasn't too well acquainted with signs, but in my book she had stepped in a gopher hole at full gallop. In her headlong haste toward happiness, I feared – as my mother used to say – her little feet were bound to trample some mighty precious things into dust.

At supper she was quiet and reserved. She toyed with her food and ate little. What food I tried to swallow seemed to lodge in my throat. From the look on her face, I knew she had made a decision and had asked herself over and over if she dared to go through with it; counting the cost and wondering about the hurts and heartaches of the aftermath.

I went to bed early and thought how fate had got us all involved; my father's uncle leaving a sandyland farm to his kin; the Cap'n surviving the war, Laura in the right place at the right time to meet him, and now this Henry Vaughn. To me came the words I had read somewhere, "We are all like wisps, and the winds of chance blow us where they will and we are sometimes powerless."

When she was ready for bed, Laura slipped into my room like a ghost, her long hair plaited down her back. Her white gown billowed around her. She reminded me of Cinderella at the Medieval Ball. She called my name softly as if she were afraid the walls had ears and would tattle. I raised myself on one elbow and looked at her there in the moonlight that came through the window, and knew she could do things to a man just by her presence and thereby take choice out of his hands.

She wanted me to drive her to the station to catch the morning train. She just had to get away. She wanted to visit friends in Shreveport. Perhaps she would find the Cap'n and return home with him the very next day. I couldn't say no, although I knew to find the Cap'n was the farthest thing from her mind. The idea rattled around in my head about this peddler. He was a powerful fast worker. It just wasn't in the cards for an inexperienced boy like me to understand the ways of a woman.

Sleep refused to come after I saw Laura there in my room, felt her nearness and smelled the perfume of her body. When day began to break beyond the pines across Laurel Creek, I rose, dressed and called to old Music.

I sat on a log deep in the woods and held my aching head in my hands. I listened to the bitch pick up the fresh scent of some wild animal; thought of the shy, hunted thing in its effort to decide which way to turn to escape. Suddenly, I realized the strange creatures of the woods had every advantage over humans. Often they could escape their troubles by running, while a human seldom could, not if he kept on living.

"I just don't understand it," I said to myself as I returned to the house and prepared to make a journey to Jubilee; a journey I felt would be the longest I would ever take in my whole life put together.

As she turned for a last look at the room where she had lain in the huge, canopied bed in her husband's arms so many nights, I thought for a moment Laura might change her mind. Suddenly she took my arm and hurried out to the buggy. She feared we might be too late to catch the train.

As we left the Big House behind, the sky was blue as the inside of a china teacup. The woods were wine-red, burnished-copper and butter-yellow. Acorns were falling on dead leaves; persimmons hung from their trees like tiny moons. The shocks of corn were teepees in the fields where the haze of Indian summer hung like the campfire smoke of dead-and-gone braves come back from far-off hunting grounds to haunt those who had so ruthlessly taken away their heritage. The wind in the pines and the monotonous drone of the crickets from the undergrowth along the road, sang a requiem to summer's going.

In spite of this beauty and brightness, the day to me was dark and ominous. In the cottonfields along the way, the negroes dragged their long sacks and pulled the cotton from the burrs in monotonous rhythm. They sang in unison the old spiritual "Keep Your Hand on the Plow; Hold on…" But how can you hold on, I thought, when everything has slipped away and left nothing to cling to?

My companion rigid, her head held high like the queen she was, remarked on the happiness of simple field hands, whose backs must ache from bending, and whose fingers throbbed from the cruel prick of the cotton burrs. "Maybe," she said sadly, "their happiness stems from the fact that somebody makes all their decisions."

"Everybody has to make decisions, even sharecroppers," I told her. I dared not look her way. I busied myself with clipping the weeds beside the road with the buggy whip. "My mother says," I continued, "that everybody has problems; a sack of rocks he carries around." She always said, "It's not the problems that get you down, but the way you handle them."

She pulled at the sleeve of my coat as much as to say, "Look at me!" Then she asked, "Do you think I am all bad because I have made a certain decision about my one big problem?" She squeezed my arm as though she would force me to say, "No!" And I knew I could not.

We rode in silence for a mile before I said, "It's not my place to judge what you do. You're a woman grown, and I'm all but a child. I once had a Sunday School teacher who told her class, 'It all depends on how bad your decision turns out to be, and how many others get hurt by it. You got to remember that if you go too far in the wrong direction, you have a hard time coming back.'" I knew, regardless of what she said, she would never let go of the idea she was a woman, and it was but natural for her to want her own children.

All at once we came to the town; the water tower glistened in the sun yonder where she would say goodbye – maybe for all time to come. She stared straight ahead with a sort of inviolate dignity, as if she were in some way out of time and space.

"Frank," she said, her voice clear as a come-to-dinner bell, "I've got my own life to live same as other people. I don't want to wither away back yonder with not even one baby to help fill that big house with laughter. Somebody said long ago, 'Nothing is good or bad, but thinking makes it so.'" I knew she was making an effort to justify what she was about to do, and was having a difficult time convincing even herself.

Then we were at the station. I tied Charley to the hitching rack before the bank. Laura went inside to cash a check. She laughed with the banker and told him she was going on a shopping spree. And for what, I wondered?

There were the stockpens that still smelled of cattle recently shipped, and yet it must have been days ago. I looked down the railroad tracks the way the train had gone with the Cap'n and tried with sheer willpower to wish him here to tell his wife she must not do what she was about to do.

The train charged into the station, and people climbed off like a bunch of monkeys and others climbed on. As I handed Laura's suitcase to the porter, I turned to her and said, my voice choking on a sob, "Oh, how I wish you didn't have to do this to the Cap'n!"

Then she was gone, her good-bye like some incredibly sad, but sweet and lingering bell. I turned unhurriedly away, blinded by tears I could not hide. I walked toward the rear of the coaches. The windows moved by as the train gathered speed. Suddenly I saw at one of them, what I hoped I wouldn't see – Henry Vaughn. Our eyes met for a fleeting moment, which was all but an eternity, and I felt anew what I had been afraid of for the past two days.

As I stood there on the platform and watched the train disappear in the distance, I wasn't there at all. Again I rode in the buggy with Laura and heard her say, "I just have to leave, Frank. Don't you see, I just can't stay here any longer and live with the thought that there will never be any children?"

I wondered what I was going to say to the Cap'n when he came home to an empty house.

# CHAPTER FOUR

The Cap'n came home that night. He rode his Maude mule all the way from Jubilee in the dark, the clop, clop of her feet came to us through the frosty stillness from the Laurel Creek bridge. As he rose up the lane, he was singing, as he was wont to do. Tonight his booming voice carried the tune of an old spiritual, "I'm Gonna Lay Down My Burden; Down by the Riverside."

I stood on the back porch and watched the moon ride high in the sky. I listened to the man on the mule and the thought came to me that he would never – not in this life – lay this newfound burden down; not by the riverside, not anywhere. Instead, he would carry it like a heavy stone on his heart all the days of his life.

Usually, on such nights, when the Cap'n rode his Maude mule into the backyard, the negroes with smoky lanterns stood back in the shadows and waited for the rush of bare feet running through the dogtrot. Down the steps and across the yard she would come like a young doe in mating season, rushing to meet her first buck.

The Cap'n would sit astride the mule until the gown-clad figure was beside him. Then he would reach down and swing her easily into his arms, to smother her with kisses, while she asked had he been gone a month? Or was it a year, and how had he been? And how perfectly perfect it was to have her man home again!

Then he would lower her to the ground and toss the sweets from his pockets into the eager hands of the wide-eyed negro children. The older negroes would rush in to welcome the Maude mule and lead her away to be curried and pampered with the usual twelve ears of corn and a bundle of fodder.

The Cap'n would sweep Laura into his arms and charge up the steps into the fireplace room. I would turn wearily, pat old Music and tell her I knew exactly how she felt; then saunter over to my room and lie awake and listen to the lovemaking across the dogtrot and wonder.

Tonight there were no little feet running to meet the Cap'n. I leaned against the porch post above the steps in my night clothes, and trembled more from the ordeal ahead than from the cold. There are moments in life when some can be a long time; others pass and are but a breath. The man on the mule sat and waited no more than a minute, but to me time ran on and on endlessly.

"Where is she? Where is she?" the Cap'n finally bellowed. The silence hung suspended in the air, while shadows from the light of the smoky lanterns made the night eerie. The negro children crept farther back in the darkness behind their parents.

Finally I heard a voice. I sounded as if it came from a well. "She's gone!" The Cap'n emitted a long sigh like an ox that had been pole-axed. He echoed the word, "Gone," three in-between-times as happens when a huge bell is tolled.

He dismounted and moved slowly and awkwardly toward the porch. I sensed a crisis building up and wanted to go away; to dash down the lane and run on and on until this cruel thing went away, or life went out of me.

He climbed wearily up the steps. I could see his face but dimly. I sensed the sternness therein, heard his loud breathing and felt the pain that seared it.

"Why did you let her go?" he demanded, like a judge who wants to know from the prisoner in court why he committed a hideous crime. He reached into the pocket of his jacket and brought out a belt. I could see the flash of the big silver buckle in the glow of the moon. I knew it was for me; the first present he had brought me in all the six months of his marriage.

He unrolled the belt and let it drop. It reminded me of an uncoiled snake. "I ought to use this on you because you let her go!" he hissed.

With a desperate lunge, I snatched the piece of leather from his grasp and flung it far into the night. In a voice I could not identify, I said, "I didn't let her go, you did!" I turned and strode to my room, slammed the door, leaned against it and shook as with a chill.

Presently, I heard the Cap'n clump through the dogtrot like one heavy with drink, or burdened with a load he could scarcely carry. I heard the latch on the front gate click. I opened the door and saw him head for the little plot where his dead rested. He might wish he, too, could take up his long sleep with his parents, but he would get no relief there from the hurt. This pain was not a stubbed toe or skinned knee a mother could kiss away the hurt of – even were she alive.

When I awoke the next morning it was raining. Not the now-and-then drops, but with a cold wind that threw the water over the tops of the trees and through the patterns of their tossing branches. There was a steady drip, drip, drip from the eaves and the trees looked drenched and desolate as they bent before the wind, shivered and righted themselves.

The house was still as a tomb. With the realization that I had overslept came one of impending doom. Where was the

Cap'n? Had he returned from the silent little city inhabited by his dead? I dressed hurriedly and hastened across the dogtrot into the fireplace room. His bed had not been slept in. I rushed into the kitchen; just then Lizzie entered from the outside to start breakfast.

"Where is he?" I asked, and noticed my voice sounded anxious, much as the Cap'n's had the night before, or was it such a short time ago? Her answer came to me as mine had to him.

"He's gone!"

"Gone!" The sound echoed and re-echoed about the room. "To find her?"

"Left long before day. Said he was goin' over to Garland county to buy cattle."

"In this rain! Why he'll come back with pneumonia!" I exploded.

"I know," Lizzie answered as she lifted the kitchen stove-lid to start a fire. "But I'm shore hit don't make him no-never-mind no more. He said with her gone, he couldn't stay here no more— ever!"

Something dark and cold settled over my thoughts. Loneliness rose and washed over me. It was all over and done with now. Everything was over but the immediate trouble the Cap'n must face and learn to live with; memories, impressions, sensations which in the end would lead to nothing and nowhere.

To the Cap'n, the tragedy of her departure is a scar across all reason, I thought, as I listened to the beat of the rain, the keening of the wind and Lizzie's breakfast preparations. I felt a chilly dark sky pressed close to the earth. Somewhere a cow mooed caressingly to her calf. A baby's cry came from the negro cabins; an old crow cawed hoarsely as it flapped drearily across the sodden pasture, and somewhere across the field, a woodpecker drilled a dead tree.

"It seems might few folks get what they want in this old world," Lizzie said, as she shoved a pan of biscuits into the oven.

I made no reply; I knew none was needed or expected. Suddenly I felt as if I had plowed a field.


The Cap'n returned at sundown. The sky had cleared; the rain was gone, but in the air was a feel of frost.

"He's wet as a drowned rat!" Lizzie exclaimed, as her husband helped lift him from the saddle and walk him into the house.

He permitted us to undress him with never a word of protest, but the look of despair on his face was terrible to behold. His eyes, slate gray, reminded me of ice on a pond. With Laura gone, he felt empty; devoid of any desire to live. The world to which he had returned so often of late, had held enchantment. Now it contained only loneliness; the enchantment gone with a tick of time.

Lizzie came with jugs of hot water and heated flat-irons to press to his feet and back. We piled high the covers and built a roaring fire in the fireplace, yet the Cap'n continued to shake like a leaf in a storm. While a negro rode for the doctor, I stood over him and hoped we would say something to help dispel the gloom which hovered in every corner of the room. Again I felt the urge to run away; to start on a long journey to where everything would be new and uncontaminated by what had happened.

## OF WHAT WAS, NOTHING IS LEFT

The doctor came that night and every night and day for what seemed like a decade, but it was only a week. For seven long days and an equal number of endless nights, the sick man lingered between staying on in the Big House or going forth to rest with his parents in the burying ground nearby.

In all that time he did not speak one word to any who waited and watched. In his deliriums he called for her. He lived and re-lived scenes and talked baby talk to her. He kept asking why she went away and when would she return?

The morning of the eighth day, he opened his eyes and asked if I had gone for the cattle he bought the week before. His words were but a whisper; his cheeks were sunken and criss-crossed with lines like a furrowed field. He said I was to go tomorrow and gather up his buys and do enough myself to finish a carload.

I looked at the drawn features, his once ruddy cheeks now pale as if drained of all blood; watched his eyes rove around the lonely bedroom and nodded. I could not trust myself to speak.

# CHAPTER FIVE

The doctor came out at noon while I was in my room reading the county weekly newspaper brought by the carrier that morning. After he left, the Cap'n sent Lizzie for me. He reached out and grasped my hand in his now fever-rid one. He said slowly, his voice indicating how weak he really was, "She's gone and we need not fool ourselves. She won't be back. I didn't tell you, but she left because I couldn't give her any children."

He paused, moved his head back and forth on the pillow and continued. "When I was on a ranch in Texas…" He paused as if embarrassed to be climbing again those hills on life's slope. "I had the mumps. I didn't take very good care of myself and before I knew it, they had gone down on me. That's why I never married before. But when I met Laura, it was different. I thought we could work out something, but her love for me couldn't offset her nesting instinct, and her unquenchable want for babies. I guess I haven't been fair to either her or myself."

For a moment his eyes burned like two coals of fire in their sunken sockets. The silence ran on and on. He squeezed my hand until the circulation stopped. Suddenly he continued. "We've got to pick up the pieces and go on. It will be like old times; just you and me. You'll stick by me, won't you, Frank?" It was the first time he had ever used my name.

He must have remembered the week-ago-night on the back porch.

"Yes," I replied. I tugged my hand from his grasp and passed it across my forehead to clear my vision, "I'll stay with you. We need each other. But it won't be like old times. My father often says that you can't draw the same water from the well twice. Besides, Laura will be back."

With much effort he raised himself to a sitting position, used his elbow for a prop and asked eagerly, "When?"

"Soon, very soon," I told him, and marveled at how he rallied at the thought. "You must hurry and get back on your feet before she gets here."

"How do you know?" he inquired anxiously. He stared at me and tried to figure out if I were some kind of magician with the power to make the impossible come to pass.

"It's a feeling I have," I said simply and hurried from the room. I did not tell him about the item in the paper which reported Mr. Henry Vaughn, who was soon to marry a prominent lawyer's daughter, had just returned from a business trip to Shreveport.

It was late evening the next day when I finished uploading cattle at Jubilee. The northbound passenger train had come and gone. As I climbed to the wagon seat, I sensed faintly the ghost of that delicate, complicated, heady perfume. Without looking, I knew Laura had come back.

And there she was. She stood by the wagon; looked up in all innocence and said, with a twinkle in her eyes, "Could a lady tramp bum a ride with a nice gentleman?"

Clumsily I stepped down to be smothered by her embrace and her, "Am I glad to be home again!" An expression which sounded not unlike the kind of greeting I had received from her long ago almost in exactly the same spot. But I knew, and she knew I knew, where she had been and what she had done. I also knew she hoped I wouldn't ask her to explain.

We were well on the way home before she asked about the Cap'n. She cried when I told her. She scourged herself as she admitted she never should have gone away. In the next breath she justified her actions by contending one had to do what one had to do; all the time she hoped I would not misjudge her motives. The more she talked, the more I came to believe – even in my youth and meager experiences – that it was not my duty to condemn or justify. Only time had the power to render such a verdict, that I fervently hoped – with crossed fingers – would be in her favor.

As the wagon crossed the rickety Laurel Creek bridge, rumbled up the lane and neared the Big House, the moon was blue-white in an almost cloudless sky. The air was warm for the time of year. A screech owl sent out his eerie call from across the pasture and the trees were noisy with the high keening of katydids.

Many of the men had sat up with the Cap'n while his wits wandered in the abyss of illness, had listened to him talk of Laura; her going away, the wherefore and why. Even the men in this strange land shut off from the rest of the world because nobody had yet conquered the scourge of distance, had little to do in their spare moments except repeat what they heard, add here and there some ideas of their own, and put words not said in the mouths of those folks who never said them.

My mind ran forward to the time when she would again ride the countryside in the rubber-tired, umbrella-topped buggy and people would stare, shake their heads and count

49

on their fingers. There were some people in the Laurel Creek community who were poor in schooling, but all of them could count. Some of the women had tongues so long they could sit in the parlor and lick grease out of the skillet in the kitchen. Laura learned all this the hard way before. She had enough spunk to come back, and I wondered if she would have what it took to stay.

Then we were at the Big House. There was Lizzie and her husband with the lantern, although the moon made everything almost light as day. When Lizzie saw who was with me, she threw up her hands and shouted, "Bless my buttons if it ain't Miz Laura!" The other negroes poured from the cabins like water from an overturned bucket. The Cap'n shouted from his bed; his Maude mule brayed from the stable, while the dog, old Music, filled the night with her loud yelps of joy.

I stayed outside and helped unhitch the team and carry in the supplies. I did not want any part of the Cap'n's greetings. Later, when he heard me in the dogtrot, he called, "Boy, you get yourself in here!" His voice sounded like one who had traveled a long ways in a dark woods and suddenly had found himself on the edge of a great moonlit meadow.

I would have given much of that night to avoid the fireplace room. Laura sat on the bed. The Cap'n was propped up by pillows. She held one of his hands in both of hers. She laughed and told him she would have him up and about soon. To her nothing had happened. It was as though she had gone for a buggy ride across Laurel Creek that very afternoon and had been late for supper.

As the Cap'n looked at her there in that quiet room that still smelled of sickness – yes, and even death – there were questions I sensed he would never ask because he really didn't want to know the answers; questions that would haunt him all the days of his life.

I watched and waited for some hint from her to him of why she left, where she had been and why she chose to come back? But none were mentioned, and I realized none ever would be by word of mouth. If she had accomplished her mission, time would take care of the answers. I wondered vaguely whether it could take care of the problems I knew were sure to come on the heels of the answers.

The days of that winter went by as days inexorably do, with their blessedly soothing routine of work, of eating and sleeping. Even before Christmas, I could tell by Laura's swollen body, the glad light in her eyes and the spring in her steps, that she had succeeded where I hoped against hope she would fail.

If the Cap'n had any inkling of what was happening, he didn't let on. All winter I avoided the fireplace room as much as possible, and never dared let him catch my eye as I noticed Laura's ever-swelling middle.

*OF WHAT WAS, NOTHING IS LEFT*

# CHAPTER SIX

While we looked the other way, spring tripped across the piney woods, dropped dogtooth violets in low places; the sky curved like a great bowl of flawless blue, and the sunshine, like a flood of golden wine, spilled over everything. When the sun set behind the pines west of the bard, its flaming splendor was a bed of pulsing embers. Then the colors began to be smoked over by night, and the stars grew in the sky like little yellow points of flame.

The Cap'n tried all too hard to be his old self again. He spent long hours astride his Maude mule. I managed to keep pace with his buying only when I swapped my bed for a lantern. It was a relief to be busy. I did not have much chance to talk with Laura, but my mind was always in a day-and-night turmoil.

If the Cap'n was busy, Laura was more so. She set hens, spent long hours making baby things she wanted to show me every time I came near the house. Her flower garden was like a bright patchwork quilt thrown down inside the yard pickets. The Cap'n chided her for working too hard, and urged her to take better care of herself. I thought maybe she kept her hands busy to take care of the thoughts that must have constantly flitted through her mind like sparrows under the barn eaves.

Where Laura had been overly anxious to make acquaintances and participate in community activities before, she now refused to budge from the Big House and its surroundings. The neighbor women came for a while, but got small comfort for their pains. To any and all questions about how are folks in Shreveport, is the town growing, and what are the latest styles in this and that, they got short, concise answers t some, and to some no answers at all.

Those who had called her "uppity" from the start had the distinct pleasure of saying, "I told you so!" It became more difficult for the Cap'n to negotiate with the men. They put a price on what they had and it was, "take it or leave it lay." His wife had withdrawn from them and the only thing they couldn't abide was being let alone. Their attitude forced the Cap'n to do his buying farther and farther away from home. My task became less glamorous and more wearisome as I jogged over mud-infested roads in winter and dusty ones in summer. The Cap'n was experiencing the leanest days of his buying and selling career.

The first week in April there was an article in the county newspaper about Henry Vaughn's wedding. I came upon Laura unawares, while she studied the picture of the bride and groom as they cut the wedding cake. I noticed the color mount on her cheeks. She sat by the window in the Cap'n's favorite ladder-backed rocking chair. She looked up from the paper and said, "He's handsome, isn't he?" I said yes and how lucky the woman was.

For a long minute she gazed out the window to where she could see the Cap'n driving a cow with a newborn calf up from the pasture, and said, "You know, Frank, every woman's got to love a bad man once or twice in her life, so she can be thankful for a good one."

The baby was born on a dark, rainy night in June. The booming voice of the Cap'n roused me from a deep pool of sleep to go for my mother, while one of the negroes went for the doctor.

As I hurried down the rutted lane, I began to think over the past three years as though I walked a road backward. The years had made me old in body and mind – much older than I cared to admit. One of the troubles with life, my mother used to say, is that you have to live it forward, even though your hindsight serves you better. I could not believe – along with some fatalists – that what is to be will be whether it ever happens or not. But if not, why had I been chosen to be caught up in the lives of two people – now there would be three – and broken on the wheel of circumstances around them? Maybe it was intended from the start for me to share their mixed-up lives and in sharing, spread their grief a little by thinning it.

How would the Cap'n take on the role of father to a child he knew was not his? As the child grew, would there be a way to shield him from the hurt when he learned who his real father was? Would not the same people who had counted so carefully on their fingers the past months, also get a certain amount of morbid satisfaction when they let the child know it was a woods colt?

When I reached Laurel Creek, a weariness seized me and I stood for a spell, listened to the waters forever flowing; the trees rustling, and thought how restful it was. I wished, with a strange of futility, that I didn't have to go farther; the baby didn't have to get born, and there was some way I could turn

55

back time to the place before Laura came. All unexpectantly, a chill wind moved across the bridge and was gone, but not before it brought the faint odor of her perfume. Then and there it came to me sadly that she was a part of our lives we could not break away from without destroying the whole.

As I lie on my bed on spring nights and hear the cry of the peepers along Laurel Creek, listen to hounds on the trail of a fox in the canebrakes, and the lonely wail of a courting whippoorwill from the thicket beyond the burying ground; over and above it all, my ears reach back across the years and I am again troubled by Laura's screams of agony that night, as I hurried my mother up the dark road to help the doctor help the baby into the world. I ponder the how and why of it all; question fate's decision to let the mother and child live that night, only to bring them to a day whose shadow would turn the world of those left into nothing save the toting of an empty sack.

The Cap'n named the baby boy Jody. He was as fine a specimen as you would ever see. From the beginning he took to life like a duck to water. His mother hovered over him the same way a hen does when she has only one chick. The Cap'n acted proud as a rooster with his first spurs. The casual observer never would have known, from the way he made over the boy, who [but what he] was the real sire.

The first time I went to haul cattle after Jody's birth, I stopped at the crossroads store to buy a pair of gloves. It had rained the night before. The creek was too muddy for fishing; the fields too wet to plow. So the menfolk in the settlement were clustered on the edge of the long store porch, where they whittled, chewed and lapped up the sunshine. The conversation ceased when I stopped by the Percherons by the roadside and headed for the store.

"How's the Cap'n's new son?" Ed Tatum, who was noted for his dirty mind and foul mouth, wanted to know.

I stopped directly in front of him. Instead of answering his question, I asked one of my own. "Do you ask because you're interested in the kid, or are you just plain nosey?"

His eyes dropped and his face lost much of its color. "You're getting' sorter uppity, too, ain't ya, boy, like the kid's Ma?"

I grabbed him by the shirt front and jerked him to his feet, and drew back my fist to slam it into his ugly face. In a flash my body went limp. My common sense told me I just couldn't fight everybody who had the same ideas I had about where Jody came from.

Trembling, I shoved the man back on the porch and hurried into the store, followed by a sigh from those who had witnessed the little scene. I knew my loss of temper would give them food for thought and talk the rest of the morning. I also felt I wouldn't be asked any more questions about the boy – not soon anyway.

The Cap'n's habits changed with the coming of the baby. More and more he depended on me to do the buying. I wondered if he was feeling old and disillusioned, or if at last he had learned there was more to life than making money.

Heretofore, the presents brought home had been for Laura. Now things were different. Jody got the presents as well as most of the attention. As soon as he was old enough to toddle, he followed the Cap'n about the place. Soon the two were almost inseparable. The boy rode the countryside astride the Maude mule in the saddle in front of the Cap'n.

To see them together, and hear the man repeat the boy's clever saying to the mother, I thought the worst was behind us unless Laura got the nesting instinct again.

After he became of school age, Laura saw but little of her son. On Saturdays he rode with the Cap'n. On Sundays they went for walks and fished from a boat on Dorcheat Lake. At night the Cap'n took the child on his knees and told him the same stories he used to tell me when I first became a member of his household. Laura felt she was on the outside looking in, but she didn't know what to do about it.

I was not surprised to have her tell me one day about how unhappy she was with an only child when she wanted at least seven. Since her scheme for having Jody had worked out so well, she hinted I might suggest how she could get a companion for him.

"Your son is not yet old enough for some busybody to tell him the Cap'n is not his real father," I told her. "So you see, you are not out of the woods as yet."

"Oh, Frank, you don't think anyone would be so cruel?" she asked with fear in her voice.

"Yes," I replied, "there are plenty of people right here in the settlement – some of them within spitting distance – who would be so cruel, as you call it. Cruel or not cruel, it could happen any time now. Don't be surprised when it does."

# CHAPTER SEVEN

There came a day in early spring when the Cap'n and Jody were far afield buying cattle. I had caught up with the hauling, and now found time to help the negroes with corn planting.

At noon Laura seemed restless and lonesome with her son and husband away. She had heard neighborhood talk about the Thompson legend ever since she had come to live at the Big House, but she had never visited the site, a half-mile down Laurel Creek from the main road. The Cap'n had refused to discuss it with her. She needed some firsthand information to collect her thoughts about this strange story. She wanted to see the pond and its surroundings. I had heard various accounts of the tragedy from several sources and offered to tell her what I knew, but preferred to hear it at the scene.

Lizzie packed a basket of food for us to eat at suppertime on the banks of the millpond because she wanted to visit her sister over beyond Burnt Bridge. The Cap'n and Jody were to be gone for the night.

The road, which led from the highway to the old mill and pond was overgrown with briers and bushes, but the curious had a well-beaten path open. We had to walk one before the other and there was little conversation from the time we left the well-traveled road until we reached our destination.

# OF WHAT WAS, NOTHING IS LEFT

We sat on rocks left from the building of the dam for the millpond. The sluice gate had been closed years ago. The long wooden trough that carried water from the dam to the huge wheel, which turned the stone to make meal and flour, had long since rotted and fallen. The water rushed over the top of the dam in a muted rumble as if singing a requiem for those who had suffered so much in the weird surroundings.

The Thompson residence, weathered, grim and unpainted, stood on a slight ridge across from a canebrake from the mill. The tall pines hard by caused it to be in shadows even in mid-day. The front porch posts had rotted and the roof was twisted and pulled from the building. It lay helter-skelter over the ground and porch floor as if tossed there by some giant's hands. The house was constructed of logs, and much of the mud chinking had been dislodged with time. It was easy to imagine piercing eyes of ghosts peering out at visitors. The old millhouse was in a sad state of decay and had become a home for varmints, snakes and owls.

The Thompsons had come to this settlement from Tennessee before the Civil War. The couple had one son; a tall, handsome, dashing lad who charmed everyone – especially the young ladies – with his looks, voice and manner. The parents were reserved, quiet and hard-working.

They brought with them millstones for grinding that proved a blessing to the settlers. Heretofore they had gone five miles to the Bug Tussle community for this service. The son and father hauled in rocks and built the dam. Neighbors came and helped with the house-raising when the logs had been hued for the residence and millhouse.

For a couple of years the miller and his son prospered. They had all the business they could do even on weekdays, for Mr. Thompson had a way with corn and wheat. He could turn out meal and flour that made better cornbread and biscuits than that brought home from the Bug Tussle mill. On Saturdays they began early and ground late. Often customers had to come back Monday to get their finished products.

Then came the Civil War. The son, now past twenty-one years of age, felt he had to go help with the fight. His father offered to hire someone to go in his stead, but the boy refused. The mother was heartbroken. The loss of her only child – even for a short period of time – was a tote-sack of misery hard for her to carry.

When the time came for his departure, the son announced to the consternation of his parents and neighbors, that he would join the Union forces. His father threatened to disown him, but the mother said if he did, she would lie down and die. A few of the settlers continued to patronize the Thompson mill, but most of them preferred to take their raw products back to Bug Tussle than give their business to a man who could not keep his son from becoming a traitor to the cause of the South.

The Thompson boy had been gone two years when word came that he had been wounded in battle. Those who had turned their back on the parents thought it served him and them right. The mother soon wasted away badly both physically and mentally. She had practically become an invalid when she learned her son was dead. She said she had nothing to live for, and was but a burden to her husband. So one night, while Mr. Thompson slept, she left her bed, crawled to the millpond and drowned herself.

After the funeral the miller packed a few things in a flour sack, and he was last seen on his way back to Tennessee where some of his kin lived. Nothing in the house or mill had been disturbed. Now there were those who claimed they had seen the ghost of the mother as she walked wearily and stumbled from the house to the mill and back. Ones who once fished in the millpond at the owner's urging, dared not go near the place, and the negroes shook as with ague at the mention of the family name.

I finished the story of this legend and turned to look at Laura. Her face was pale in the gathering dusk; her brow knitted in thought, as she plucked at the dogtooth violets that jutted from the edge of the rocks where she sat.

"You know," she finally said with a sigh and a whisper, as if afraid the ghost of the drowned woman might be listening, "I can sympathize with the mother. If anything should ever happen to my son, I don't think I could go on living either. It's a terrifying thought."


It is said that a mule is so plague-taked mean that he will act like a gentleman for twenty years just to get to kick your brains out before he dies. When Jody was twelve, one of the pissle-tailed mules, that had pulled a plow for my father all the years he had spent in the Laurel Creek settlement, ran away. My father was thrown from the wagon and injured to such an extent that he never left his bed again. Two months later he died.

All my brothers and sisters had gone from the sandyland farm to jobs in town. So there was little left for me to do but go home and take over the farm and care for my mother. The Cap'n swore while Laura and Jody cried. I tried to tell them it wasn't as if I were going a thousand miles; that I would likely see them most every day. But Laura argued it wouldn't be the same. I didn't say so, but I knew it hadn't been the same for a long, long time, and regardless of what happened, it would never be the same again.

My bed in the Big House was hardly cold before Laura's cousin, Cindy, moved in to start sleeping in it. If coming events cast their shadows before them, her arrival was an omen.

Cindy was like her cousin only in her striking beauty. She laughed easily where Laura seldom even smiled. She was vivacious and optimistic. Everything, she insisted, happened for the best. She admitted that the world was thorn-infested, but insisted that the roses smelled mighty sweet. She had just finished her schooling and was a full-fledged trained nurse. She was highly amused at Lizzie's answer to a neighbor's question, "What does Miz Cindy do?"

"I don't know for shore," Lizzie replied, "but I think she's a nuss' on de train!"

Words proved futile when folks started out to describe this visitor. She was a tall, willowy woman a little past first youth. There was an easy grace about her that reminded me of a young filly. She had a way of talking with her hands, her gestures saying as much as the words she clipped off with great easy. Her eyes crinkled in their sockets and were much like the liquid pools in Laurel Creek. There was little vanity about her; just enough to make her more interesting.

Jody, childlike, was captivated by what he called his brand-new cousin. He begged to stay home from school just to be with her; a privilege he had not asked for in regards to trips with the Cap'n.

At the end of one week of Cindy's stay, Doctor Jordon was called to see Lee Dorsey's home in Cracker's Neck to attend Lemuel, a boy the age of Jody and his playmate. After the preliminary examination, the doctor turned from the sick bed and shook his head sadly. Lemuel had a disease that rapidly spread terror in any community – typhoid fever. He called upon Cindy to help him ferret out the cause. First they looked for the culprit in a sample of water from the school well. And, there it was!

The school was closed. Laura was frantic. Jody had played with Lemuel the day before he became ill. Now she had a feeling her son would be the next victim. She kept him in the house, and shielded him from all contact with anybody; and this included the Cap'n and me.

Little Lemuel Dorsey grew steadily worse. Cindy, against Laura's admonition, gathered up her belongings and moved into the Dorsey home. Laura appealed to the Cap'n and me to try and talk sense into the nurse's head. But we both agreed it was a noble gesture.

In spite of all the doctor and nurse could do, Lemuel died within a week. Cindy was beside herself with grief. It was her first case, and little Lemuel was too young to die. Jody had begged to go visit the sick boy, but that was out of the question. Now he wanted to attend the funeral to take a farewell look at one who had meant so much to him. However, Laura would not hear of to it.

Five other school children came down with the fever before it ran its course. Cindy went from house to house doing what she could. She sat for hours without sleep and administered to children she had learned to love. She suffered with each patient and each parent when the battle seemed lost. In her suffering, she often wondered if she would ever make a very efficient nurse. But the doctor called her another Florence Nightingale.

Laura was positive her cousin acted the part of a very foolish woman, but she got no sympathy for her views from anybody. "Laura has always been a very selfish person,"

Cindy said to me one night, as we sat beside the bed of a child with a burning fever. "She's an only child. Her parents were well-to-do, and they carried her around on a silver platter as she grew up. When she lost them, she acted as if she were the only one who ever had trouble strike. She has always been a great one to find out what she can't have, and immediately decide that that is what she wants most. She will never be happy because she has no way of adjusting to life. She doesn't know how to fight in times of trouble that all mankind seems heir to."

No other children died of the typhoid scourge. The doctor and parents agreed wholeheartedly that all of them were pulled through by Cindy's careful, tender and loving administration. "She just wouldn't let them die," the doctor said.

Doctor Jordon and the typhoid epidemic convinced Cindy that her place was here among these simple people who did not know what to do in an hour of uncertainty except to pray and hope. I had fallen deeply in love with this remarkable woman and was highly elated over her decision. It is indeed "an ill wind that blows nobody good," I thought.

*OF WHAT WAS, NOTHING IS LEFT*

# CHAPTER EIGHT

Soon after the typhoid epidemic was over, the Cap'n and Laura permitted Jody to ride Charley and go with a group of other neighborhood boys to an afternoon performance of a circus in Bussey. He did not return home that night, but sent the horse home by one of his companions. He had decided to join the circus. The next morning the Cap'n sent for me to accompany him to bring the boy back.

I found Laura pacing the floor of the dogtrot in the Big House, her face pale and drawn; her eyes red and swollen from weeping and the lack of sleep. She and the Cap'n must have had words. He sat on the porch edge, his eyes pointed toward the graves in the little enclosure hard by. The light in those sockets burned less brightly than I had seen them since his illness. He did not appear to notice me as I mounted the steps and stood before Laura. She was rigidly erect, as I had seen her so often as of late. Pain ran through her words as she begged me to please hurry home and get the Cap'n on the way to bring her boy home.

Cindy, who was readying her things to go with Doctor Jordon on a "granny" case beyond Britt Crossing, paused in her preparation as Laura asked, "Why, oh why would he do such a thing?"

"If you ask me," Cindy said in that gay voice of hers, "what is there to get excited about? Why, to join a circus is

67

a part of every boy's growing up. I used to wish I were a boy so I could join one."

"But he's never been away from home overnight before!" Laura explained.

"There may be the answer to your problem – if there is a problem. Maybe the kid suffered a mild case of 'apron-string-strangulation!'" Cindy retorted.

Laura paused in her pacing long enough to tell her cousin, "You have never been a mother, therefore you are not qualified to judge!"

"But I've been a sister, and I know my brother did some strange things, even though running away to join a circus wasn't one of them. If he had, I think I would have understood."

"That's different," Laura argued. In the next breath, she wondered if Jody was still disturbed because he was not allowed to attend Lemuel's funeral. I didn't tell her so, but I had an inkling this behavior of his had nothing whatsoever to do with Lemuel.

As we hurried out to the buggy, I asked of the Cap'n, "Why do you think the boy ran away"?

He stopped dead still, looked back the way we had come as if he had left something behind that he needed. Then he shook his head like a fighter who had been all but knocked out in the ring. "I wish I was sure it wasn't because of what I think it is," he said.

The day was one I wish I could forget. Things had a chill gray anonymity. The fields and trees blurred and ran together like my thoughts. These two people – so much alike in their pride – were bound to break sooner or later because they could not bend. They believed to bend was just another way to show weakness; the one force that would never bring either of them to capitulate. For a brief time they had marched hand in hand toward happiness. Now they were out of step; each seemed to be responding to a different drummer.

The Cap'n was silent for a long time after we put Charley in the road and hurried him toward Bussey. There we would take the train to Texarkana, where the circus was showing. Finally he said, choosing his words carefully; words he would never say to another, words he never thought he would say to me. "It was a mistake from the start. We shouldn't have married – ever."

"Are you sure?" I asked. I tried to be casual.

"Yes," he said very slowly. "I'm quite sure."

"Just when did you make this startling discovery?"

As we crossed the Burnt Bridge over Dorcheat Creek, the wooden boards rattled too loud for conversation. I studied my companion in the absence of words, only to find he had seemingly grown old while I looked the other way. His face was dusted with a deep-running weariness he appeared unable to brush off.

With the bridge behind us and Charley again urged on at a rapid trot by the whip in the Cap'n's hand, he said suddenly without looking at me, "It must have been the night she came home from Shreveport where she had gone to find a father for her child."

"Then," I asked, although I knew the answer, "why didn't you send her away?"

"I just couldn't!" His voice broke and he shook his head sadly.

69

"You couldn't, or were you just too proud to admit your mistake?"

"I didn't know she was pregnant!" It was as if his voice came from afar off.

I knew my advice or any admonition I gave would blow past his ears like wind, but I had to say what I had to say. I felt so helpless. My wisdom was so limited in comparison to his. Why did I have to be leaned upon when I should be the leaner?

"Cap'n," I said as I chose my words very carefully, "in my bringing up, my parents told their youngsters that when the going got rough we'd just have to bite the bullet and hang on. Pa often said the only strength a man had was in himself. You have no choice expect to live with what you have whether it was a mistake or not. You'll just have to make the best of it. The matter of choice was taken out of your hands a long time ago. Maybe it was when you had the mumps, or when you decided to marry Laura and not tell her you had no seed with which to give her children."

I paused while time stretched forward and carried us helplessly toward our meeting with Jody. My companion rode with his head down, the lines slack in his gnarled hands. I summoned a strength I didn't know I possessed, and continued. "The past is water under the bridge, and you can no more recall it than you can make Laurel Creek flow backward to where it came from. You can run from your mistake – if a mistake it was – but you can't run far enough. We'll bring the boy back, and life will go on in the Big House. It can't be the same, but it will go on. There's no way to stop it this side of the grave."

Little more was said between us until we entered the circus grounds in Texarkana, where the crew was getting ready for the night performance. The circus manager said he had hired a boy of Jody's description that afternoon. The boy had refused to divulge his name. In fact, he said he didn't have a name, since he didn't know who his father really was.

The Cap'n winced at that, and drew his hand wearily across his face as if he had been slapped. He advised the man that the boy did have a mother who was concerned about him. As his guardian, he had come to take the boy home.

We found Jody carrying water to the elephants; the one-time dream of every youngster. He promptly informed the Cap'n he was not about to go home. "You're not my father, and you can't make me!" he shouted.

The blow was too much for the Cap'n. He stumbled weakly to a bale of hay and collapsed on it his head in his hands, his body a-tremble. His reason struggled against this moment he had come to dread since the first day he noticed Laura's swollen belly.

With a start, he seemed to reach back and gather strength from the past experiences of making decisions in battle and on cattle drives. His change in demeanor reminded me of the times he had told me about thirsty cattle getting the smell of water. "Young man," he asked, his voice strong with decision, "who says I'm not your Daddy?"

"They all say it!"

"'They Say' are the biggest liars in the world. Now you listen to me. You're going home right now and no more of your sass! Do you hear me? It wouldn't take too much for me to lam the tar out of you!"

I had fished Laurel Creek with this runaway. We had
hunted together in the fall. In summer we had swum in the
Thompson Millpond and speculated about the ghost that
was said to haunt the surroundings. I had made his first willow whistle and taught him how to blow a tune on it. He had
ridden miles and miles with me behind the Percherons, and
helped load cattle like a man. He had never refused to do
my bidding. I knew well he worshipped the Cap'n, had spent
hours with him as they rode three counties on the Maude
mule. He had proudly called him Dad.

Now I looked at him as he stood rigid and defiant. His
eyes blazed; his fists were clenched. I turned away to hide
my emotions. When I looked again at his tear-stained face,
I realized he never again would be a little boy. He was now
a child-man. He struggled with a problem so much bigger
than he was and one he had not made. This is the end of the
line, I thought, this is where everybody gets off. I was glad
the one who had destroyed this little fellow's world was not
present – I could have killed him with my bare hands.

The enraged little boy-man made the mistake of looking
at me. His chin trembled. The rage went out of him as I
had seen the ice in the far-off Ohio in the spring. The next
instant he was clinging to me; his body shook with violent
sobs, his world shattered in a million pieces at his feet.

There was little said on the long journey home, for what
was there to say? Laura was overcome with joy. As she
hugged Jody, she asked over and over, "Why did you do it?"
But he did not try to answer his mother's question, and I
knew he never would.

# CHAPTER NINE

In the days that followed our trip to Texarkana – whenever winter borrowed a day from spring and I could spare the time from the ever-pressing tasks on the farm – Jody and I rose the countryside on Charley and a prancing Pinto filly the Cap'n bought for him. But the boy was not the same. He talked little. Always he seemed to think about something not connected with the two of us. Often I found his gaze turned toward the far horizon, as if he tried to see something that was not there.

He had finished the eighth grade and no longer could attend the Laurel Creek school. His mother sent away for books and tried to teach him at night. But she said that she could not keep his attention. Suddenly, in the midst of a problem, or in his reading, he would get up and wander out into the yard. When he came back, he would complain of a headache and escape to his room.

"I just can't understand it!" Laura said to me many times. I could have told her plenty, but I held my tongue. I knew what was said could not be unsaid. What was done was done, and nothing said or done could change it.

One day, while we were fishing in the Thompson Mill-pond, Jody quite casually remarked, "You know, Frank, I think I'll go away to school."

"Well," I replied as calmly as I could, "your mother would miss you no end, but I'm sure she would be pleased."

But it didn't work. The boy must have enrolled in a half-dozen schools within the next four years. He would come home for a space between schools, rip around the country on his mare, flirt with the girls at play parties; get drunk and fight. He dared anybody to challenge his right to rudeness and to do as he damned pleased.

The Cap'n's Maude mule was getting old – along with her master. One morning, when he needed to ride across the country, she was lame. The Cap'n decided to ride the Pinto instead.

That night the mare came home, but her saddle was empty. For two days and three nights we searched every road and made inquiry at every house where the Cap'n might have passed. Early the third day we found him. The pony had evidently shied, thrown her rider from the saddle and then bolted. He was apparently unconscious and had crawled a quarter of a mile into the woods. We brought his broken, all but lifeless body home, and waited for him to die.

For six long months he hovered between living and going to lie with his parents in the little plot where I found refuge so often in this crisis, and while I pondered the unceasing effort of fate to break this man. Inside this body, now so much like a great oak felled by the winds in a violent storm, the embers of life still burned ever so feebly. It was Cindy, I knew, who kept the faint – and at times indistinguishable – glow from turning to ashes. At times when we thought he had gone away, she called him back. Only her voice soothed him whenever pain fought to possess his now frail body.

Laura seldom left the Cap'n's side night or day. She sent for Jody, who had recently enrolled in another school. She tried to make a man out of him. She thought the Cap'n's illness might goad him to buy and haul cattle as we had done for so long. But she had waited too long. They do say the time to start rearing a child is a hundred years before he is born.

The boy took some of the Cap'n's scant savings and, over his mother's protest, bought a model-T. He went helling through the three counties where the Cap'n had ridden his Maude mule so proudly. He made his mother believe he was doing all right at the game his predecessor had played so well so long.

I learned through my mother that those who loved to gossip told how he "bigged" three girls while the Cap'n was fighting for his life. He spent money going and coming, and got it, folks thought or imagined, by running whiskey for a moonshiner.

Jody would disappear for a week at a time, while Laura paced the floor from the Cap'n's bedside to the front porch to watch for him. She grew thin; the tired look was always in her eyes. We tried to prevail on her to rest. She would not because she could not. She lived in little cracks of time, aware only momentarily of what went on around her. She was all dry inside, so she could get no relief from weeping.

One fine spring day, the erring playboy wrecked the car and all but killed a female companion of questionable reputation. His mother refused to mortgage the farm, so he was forced to take the saddle again.

Now he was home nights. He shut himself in what had been my bedroom. He seldom spoke to anybody, not even his mother. In the daytime he took to the woods and left us to wonder.

One blustery, rainy day, I tailed him to see where he spent his time. I all but got myself filled with lead when I walked up on his moonshine still, deep in the canebrakes on Laurel Creek near the old Thompson tumbled-down residence.

"Nice setup, eh?" he remarked. "Nobody will ever find my still here; they're too scared of old Mrs. Thompson's ghost."

My loud and long protests were ignored as he went about cooking off a setting of mash. I was told in no uncertain terms to mind my own business – if I had any. I was also advised to keep my big mouth shut. How else, he wanted to know, could he make a quicker buck to buy medicine for an old man who was no kin of his, and keep bread and meat on the table for a slut like his mother?

I promptly knocked him down for the slur and hoped to slam some sense into his worthless head. He got up, rubbed his chin and insisted I needn't waste time and effort on somebody who wasn't worth it.

"You can say that again!" I told him. Then I went on to say I would take my chances on that score if he would only go home with me and forget about this unlawful way to fulfill obligations he had not been so excited about before.

I stayed with him until the ugly day spent itself and night took over. We walked home together, but I did not get any promises. He was not interested in the law-abiding angle of the question. He was old enough to make up his own mind and was beholden to nobody.

My mother died in her sleep that night. Jody attended the funeral, but he did not speak to me, and I was glad. Laura took time from her worries over her husband and son to do what she could for me. She found tears she didn't know she had, to weep over my mother's death. She stayed for a while after the funeral to help get things in their proper places in the lonely house that would never again be home to me. She insisted I move back to the Big House. I promised to give it some thought, but I knew that to go back from this to that would be like jumping out of the frying pan into the fire.

Cindy insisted that we get married so she could help look after me and the farm. But before our plan materialized, tragedy struck again at the Big House.

*OF WHAT WAS, NOTHING IS LEFT*

# CHAPTER TEN

One week from the day my mother was buried, revenue officers surprised Jody at his still. He made a run for it. In the exchange of gunfire, he was wounded. He managed to get to the old Thompson house, where he holed up and swore he would never surrender. He called for the officers to send in the dirty bastard who turned him in. He wanted to have the pleasure of blowing my brains out.

I was at the Big House when one of the men came to see if there was anyone to go plead with the boy to give up. They didn't want to kill him, but had to capture him whether they killed him or not. The Cap'n had improved some and sat on the front porch in his rocking chair. The rest of us were in the kitchen.

The stillness was broken by a loud voice that called for me to saddle his Maude mule. Memory fails me when I try to recall all that happened. I helped the Cap'n to mount the mule while Laura protested he would kill himself. I remember he told her it was a little late to worry about that and assured her it would make little or no difference.

The old man had little strength, but enough lay buried behind his burned-out eyes and deep within that once huge frame of his – now wasted to pale skin stretched over tired bones –to pick up the bridle reins, and urge his old and stumbling Maude mule into a slow, running walk.

## OF WHAT WAS, NOTHING IS LEFT

I paced beside the mule, my hands on the reins to keep her from stumbling and held to the Cap'n's thin leg to keep him in the saddle. I could feel his knobby knee as he urged his mount on. In my mind's eye, I could see him again in his youth as he rode straight in the saddle and proudly took orders from Teddy. And I wondered where the years had gone.

Today the rider did not take orders from anyone. As we came upon the officers who stood guard, they asked if he knew what a risk he was about to take. I don't believe he even heard them. He looked down at me and inquired, "Why are we stopping here? Let's get on to the boy." The voice seemed to come from a giant of other days, when the hot blood of younger years coursed through a strong and ruler-straight body.

As we neared the weather-beaten house, he stopped the mule. He reached down and placed his bony hand on my head. For a thin, soundless second of time, I was a fourteen-year-old boy again; a frightened lad, recently hired to drive a team for a man who was a physical giant and a god, sent from high among the Olympian clouds for the sole purpose of making me happy.

I was brought back to the present by the low voice of the man on the mule. "If you don't mind, boy, I'd like to take it from here."

"But you may get shot!" I protested.

"If that young scamp shoots me and I ever find it out, there'll be the Devil to pay. Don't you worry; he's not going to shoot me."

I took my hand from his scrawny leg, looked up into his eyes, gave him a salute and said, "Good luck, Sir." He was so weak he could scarcely raise his hand; but he touched his forehead, and a smile came slowly to his tired mouth. Then

I stepped back and watched him plow through the canes toward the old house, like a ship on the high seas.

I hurriedly turned my back and walked a little ways. I expected to hear the shot that would topple the old patriarch from his saddle. But no blast broke the stillness. The next sound I heard was a loud cry of anguish from the throat of the Cap'n.

I rushed to the door of the house and saw the old man seated on the floor with Jody's head on his lap. He tenderly stroked the boy's forehead – now damp with death. Jody clung to him and cried, "I'm sorry, Dad! Tell Mother I'm so sorry."

And then the Cap'n's voice, like a mother talking to a sick child, "It's all right, son. Your old Dad understands."

"Your hands are so warm," the boy sobbed, "and I've been cold so long!"

We saw a tremor pass over the boy's body. Then a mist crawled up out of the canebrake. The frogs chorused. We heard Laurel Creek as it tumbled over the dam, and it was midnight inside me. We heard the wind sough mournfully through the trees and the voice of the Cap'n as he wept like King David of old at the death of his son Absalom, "Oh, my son! My son!" The officers hurriedly reached for their hats and there was not a dry eye among them.

The Cap'n asked to carry Jody's body home on the Maude mule. I was sent ahead to break the news to his mother. She stood on the porch and shaded her eyes from the late afternoon sun. She was such a lonely figure in a world so full of the holes of loneliness that it was difficult to step around them.

As I closed the gate behind me and turned to face her, she asked, her voice hardly more than a whisper, "He's dead, isn't he?" Her inquiry was more statement than question. Her mother instinct had told her before I had the chance.

Wearily I nodded my head and tried not to look at her. I fought to close my eyes against the agony of her face; a cameo of despair, a picture that was to follow me all the days of my life.

I thought she was going to faint. She bent her head to stay the swirling. She reached out one hand to grasp a porch post to steady herself. Suddenly she jerked her sagged shoulders erect, brushed a wisp of gray hair from her face and said, "Come, Frank, and tell me all about it." With that she walked through the dogtrot to the door of Jody's room. And, at that moment, the picture in the history-book of Queen Antoinette of France, as she walked to the guillotine, flashed through my mind.

In a halting, stumbling voice, my throat clogged with wonder at her calmness, I told her all that happened and was said between the Cap'n, her boy and me, from that long-ago day we had driven out of the yard in the buggy to make the long ride to Texarkana. But, I felt as I went along that she did not listen. She heard voices which were not in the room. She relived scenes foreign to the ones I tried to show her.

The story finished, I sat before her and held one of her cold hands in both of mine. I tried to make her believe all that happen, somehow happen for the best. We heard the Cap'n on the porch; then the slow tread of the officers' feet as they bore the body across the dogtrot. The tired voice that directed them into the fireplace room called out for me.

Still Laura did not move. She sat as though she had turned to stone. I rose, touched my lips to her forehead – which was as cold as marble – patted her shoulder and left the room, closing the door softly behind me.

The officers had placed Jody on the Cap'n's bed and taken their leave. They left behind a house full, a yard full and our hearts full of misery. But the law had been upheld; they had done their bounden duty. Now they would move to new locations, and later they would remember buy vaguely the day when their lives crossed ours.

*OF WHAT WAS, NOTHING IS LEFT*

# CHAPTER ELEVEN

It took a long time to prepare Jody's body for burial. The Cap'n locked the doors to the room and refused to answer any knocks. Throughout the ghastly ordeal, he bent over the body and mumbled incoherently. He told the lump of clay too late that everything would be all right. Well, I knew everything hadn't been all right from the day the boy was conceived, and everything would be never all right again.

When I finished my ablutions, I took the Cap'n by the hand and let him to the kitchen. I put food before him, but knew he would not eat. I went back to Jody's room and found Laura had not moved since I left her. Cindy had tried to put her to bed, but without success. Her grief had hypnotized her; she seemed to be in a trance. A numbness had fallen upon her and made her immune to any feeling.

Without a word, I took her in my arms and carried her across the dogtrot into the room where her dead son lay. I noticed how thin she had become; how frail, as if a gust of wind would carry her away. I placed her in the Cap'n's chair beside the bed and quietly left her alone with her dead son.

Soon I heard her weeping. Her grief came in a great self-accusing flood, her loud lamentation like that of the mother of the firstborn crying in Egypt after the death angel had passed. Her sobs ran through the house and spilled over into the yard, where the negroes heard them and started an eerie wailing that sounded like lost souls winging their way through an outer darkness.

"Now the flood gates are open," I thought, as I listened to Laura. "She'll get relief from the numbness of her grief." Later I went in to find her weeping without sound, the tears falling on the face of her son.

The neighbors came. They brought food and stayed to help eat it. They made a Roman holiday of the occasion. They took more away than they brought in beholding grief and it not their own.

"Would we bury him in the family plot?" Laura wondered.

The Cap'n answered angrily, "Where else is there to bury our boy?"

Throughout the night they held a vigil by the bed where Jody lay. They held each other's hands and said little. What was there to be said? They stared at the naked walls and, like the slow ticking of the old clock on the mantle, they asked over and over, "Why? Why? Why?" If there was an answer, they came no closer to finding it than did Eve when she held Abel's lifeless head on her lap.

Some were bold enough to ask me about digging the grave, but the look on the Cap'n's face warned them not to direct any interrogation his way. He sat immobile, looked off into space or paced from dogtrot to kitchen to fireplace room, and back again.

Although curiosity demanded they look at the body, none had the courage to attempt to open the door behind which lay the tragic figure. None was strong enough to force himself to offer a soothing word or a tender clasp of the hand to either the Cap'n or Laura.

Ed Tatum came and wanted to go to Bussey for the coffin. He needed, he reasoned, to do something to make amends for all the unkind things he said about the boy. Grudgingly, I bade him go, and thought surely somebody should be allowed to garner something worthwhile from all this.

I asked about a preacher for the graveside service. I could tell by the expression on both their faces that they did not want anybody to say anything. But the decision was mine. I did not feel it would be right to send Jody away without even a prayer, and there was none in me.

It was a bleak, overcast day, with intermittent rain that blew in feeble gusts across the field that surrounded the open grave. It was as though the heavens saw fit to weep with and for those who had asked only for the bread of happiness and were given a stone instead. The wind whined, and the trees moaned and solemnly honed their limbs.

The curious from three counties were there. They overflowed the yard, the burial plot and reached across the surrounding field. There were those who had joked and laughed with the Cap'n, and many who had called Laura and her sons names; their faces drawn and unsmiling. They stood helplessly by and hoped someone would ask them to do something to ease their shame for words they had said and thoughts they had thought.

"There are some black spots in the life of the one who lies before us," Preacher Biglow said, "but let him who is without sin cast the first stone. He is in the hands of a merciful God who understands all the causes for both our sinning and our goodness. May He be merciful to this boy, who was cut down so young, and to those who are left to mourn his untimely departure from this life.

"And may this tragedy cause all of us to examine our lives, and may we make a special effort to root out the evils that have caused this hour to come to pass. Someday we'll understand, but until then, we have to trust in the One who notices even the fall of the sparrow."

The wagon lines I had drawn over the backs of the Percherons so often were used to lower the casket into the grave. Then the shovels were brought forward and the clods began to fall on the box. They were like the blows of sledgehammers that beat on my brain. I was filled with thoughts that flitted here and there like disturbed bats in a cave.

"Ashes to ashes," intoned the preacher. "In my Father's house are many mansions. If it were not so, I would have told you ...." Sounds of guns exploding in a canebrake. ... Sowing and reaping; reaping and sowing. ... Negroes chanting in a cottonfield. ... The sound of drums, and the Cap'n charging up the hill with soldiers dying around him. ... The band playing at the circus. ... Train wheels whirring, turning but going nowhere. ... a face at a window, and a little boy piping a tune on a willow whistle. ... Bluebirds of happiness dead in their nests.

"Let not your hearts be troubled...." Unshed tears in eyes like pits of gray granite; tears in dark pocketed eyes. ... Pain riding faces. ... A galloping pale horse whose rider's name is death. ... Clods falling, shovels clanging and boards on Laurel Creek bridge echoing a frosty morning. ... The faces of my dead-and-gone parents. ... A baby's reaching arms. ... A dying boy gasping "I've been cold for so long!" A open grave, a cruel mouth across the face of the burying ground.

The crowd slowly dispersed, wonder and disappointment on many faces because the casket had not been opened for a last long look at the husk of Jody; a husk robbed of its kernel by the blight of gossip. Some were bold enough to ask me why they were not granted this accustomed privilege. I told them it was a request made by Cap'n, and left them to wonder. He did not want the one who had destroyed the boy, by telling him who his father wasn't, to see the results. It might give the teller a false sense of pride at his accomplishment if he were to look upon his handiwork.

When we had done all that could be done, we left the Cap'n and Laura sitting in ladder-backed chairs by the long, ugly mound that was like a gash across the small enclosure. Nobody – not even the preacher – tried to lift their veil of despair from their faces with words of sympathy.

*OF WHAT WAS, NOTHING IS LEFT*

# CHAPTER TWELVE

I could not return to the gloom-shrouded house. I turned from the burying ground and started across the field edged by scrubby pines, old Music at my heels. We would bury ourselves in the woods. Maybe she would find a rabbit, I thought, while I tried to find a way; a direction to go from here.

We had just reached the clearing's edge when I came face to face with Henry Vaughn. Not his presence, but his face was a shock. "You had no right to come," I said angrily. "You knew you weren't wanted!"

"I had to come to show respect for my son. I'm sorry about it all," he said weakly.

"You are all of twenty years too late," I told him vehemently. "You should have thought about all this then."

"That is all I have thought about for so many years. It has all but driven me out of my mind and wrecked my health. I'm a sick man – not long for this world."

"Maybe you are getting your just desserts." My hand was on the slender bough of a small pine. I stripped the needles from the branch and flung them into the wind with a feeble gesture of resignation. "If only I had killed you the first time I set eyes on you!"

"It would have been a blessing," he told me. "My wife re-
fuses to bear me a child. She is insanely jealous and married
me only because the one who could have given her a place
in high society jilted her. I didn't know this at the time I married her. She never had a thought for anybody but herself. I
have gone through enough misery to supply the whole world.

Memory cut away the years, and time was lost as we stood
and faced each other. A sudden sharp stab of pain caused
him to gasp for breath. There was a taste of brass in my
mouth, as I said slowly, "A long time ago some wise man
said, 'The mills of the gods grind slowly, but they grind
exceedingly small.' Maybe it is wrong of me, but I'm glad
you are miserable. I know you are not altogether to blame,
but you had a very large part in bringing about the misery
of this day to all of us. I wish I could feel sorry for you, but
I don't. I only feel contempt. If we ever meet again, I'll kill
you for the yellow cur you are." I turned from him and fled
into the woods, the catch of a sob in my throat.


Time has been kind enough to erase from my memory much
of what followed immediately on the heels of Jody's funeral.
The lives of those in the Big House were like a jigsaw puzzle
accidentally brushed from the table of living – the parts scattered to the winds. The Cap'n tried, in his feeble way, to pick
up the pieces and put them back in place. But the biggest
piece of all was missing, and the jagged edges of the others
stuck out like the top of the garden palings.

The negroes tried to face up to the crisis, but now they
came to the Cap'n and begged permission to leave. They
were visited nightly, they said, by Jody's ghost. He haunted
their dreams, and often came to stand beside them in the
barn when they went to do the chores.

The Cap'n bade them go, and one by one they left; their household goods piled high on borrowed wagons, the women followed behind on foot, and chanted incoherently with backward looks to see if they were followed by what they feared.

There came a day when Laura refused to eat. She insisted on spending her daylight hours sitting in an old rocking chair I had placed at the head of her son's grave. If she must stay there all day, I reasoned, she might as well be comfortable in a physical way. As night closed in, her cousin and I went out to the enclosure and lifted her tenderly by each arm and walked her to the house. She never protested, but the look on her face was terrible to see. When we put her to bed, she favored us with a wan smile that was little short of a grimace.

"Luckily, she does not feel anything. She has nothing left to feel with," her cousin said.

One day Laura stayed in her room until noon, then asked me to go with her to see Jody. She had talked with him the night before, she said, and he was all right. The conversation made her very happy. She ate a hearty meal with us and remarked at how sorry she was to have been so reserved and so much trouble lately. When she was ready to go, she went to the Cap'n, put her hands on his shoulders and kissed his forehead. "Forgive me, dear, for all the trouble I've caused you," she said.

On the way to the rocking chair she walked proudly erect, and had a grip on my arm that was painful. She thanked me time and again for all I had done to help everybody. As I started to go, she took my hand and pulled me to her. She embraced me and tears came in her eyes as she said, "Goodbye, Frank. Be good to yourself and Cindy. She has grown very fond of you."

"I'm so glad you are much better," I told her. "Everything is going to work itself out and you and the Cap'n will be the same as you were long ago." I whistled a note of happiness as I left her – a note that expressed how pleased I was with the turn of events.

Late in the afternoon I returned from work and noticed the chair was empty. I was elated with the thought that Laura had gone to the house unassisted and before the usual time.

"I thought she was still out there," Cindy said. "I haven't felt too well and have spent most of the afternoon in bed. I'm sure she hasn't been in the house."

I ran through the dogtrot and out the front gate, my mind seething with the thoughts of all that transpired at noon. In the dust of the road, I noticed her footprints pointing toward Laurel Creek. Now I knew what I should have been aware of when she was so solicitous with her goodbyes.

"Oh no! Oh Jesus, no! No! No!" my voice trailed away as I rushed down the road.

I knew just where to go. All her noon gaiety was to cover up what she intended to do. I raced the mile to the pond without any feeling other than the wind rushing past my ears. At the pond's edge, I paused long enough to notice her fresh footprints and to shuck off my shoes. I dived into the cold water. In the glow of the last light from the sun before it dipped behind the towering pines and with the darkened deep of the millpond, I saw her face. It was framed by her hair that moved with the wafts of the undercurrent. Was she smiling at something her son said to her the night before, or had she heard him calling to her from the Elysian Fields beyond the

94

Shores of Death? The undertow moved. Or was her brow creased in suffering because life had lost all its meaning when Jody went away?

I refused to attend the funeral. There would be too many of the curious. Their stares might drive me to do or say something I shouldn't. Besides, I wanted to remember her as she was before she decided she was called to join her son and must answer by doing what she did.

Anyway, hadn't I attended her funeral long ago? To me, she died one bright October day when the world was clothed in scarlet; while crows cawed from the tops of pines in the bottoms, and the sound of sing-songing negro spirituals swelled from the cotton rows along the road to Jubilee.

OF WHAT WAS, NOTHING IS LEFT

# CHAPTER THIRTEEN

The next morning when the Cap'n came in to breakfast, I was cleaning and oiling the pistol he kept handy to shoot hawks that bothered the chickens.

"Going hunting?" he asked casually.

"Yes," I told him. "Skunk hunting."

"Then you know who he is?" he asked, matter-of-factly.

"Yes, I've known all along. I wish to God I didn't!"

"Don't do it, boy," he said sternly. "You may not think we've had enough trouble, but I do. After all," he stopped and found his place at the table and started to toy with his fork, "he gave us years of pleasure we would not have had if he had not fathered Jody. Please let sleeping dogs lie. Let there be no more pulling and prying and poking, and this never letting some things alone."

"Pleasure is not all he gave us," I told him sadly. "Do you think for a minute the joy outweighs the misery; the laughing ever near balancing the weeping? Is what he did worth the loss of two people we love?"

He dropped his eyes to the plate and made no attempt to answer. So I went on. "Somebody has this job to do. It should be you, but you don't have the will or the strength."

I put the gun in my inside coat pocket, rose and stood for a long time and looked down at the man who had had so much to do with molding my character. All the years I had lived under his roof and the sound of his voice flashed before me like a motion picture on a huge screen.

I turned and gazed out the window to the fields where a short time ago the hands had toiled and tilled; had tickled the soil with hoe and plow, while they sang and shouted in the joy of work they did for the Cap'n. Now all that was gone on the wind of tragedy and over the hills of time. Yet, the man who had played the lead role in all this, sat there and talked about how much pleasure he had garnered from it all.

The fields lay barren like the inside of the Big House. "No man," I heard myself say to nobody and nothing, "has a right to do what he did. Maybe it is not my duty to try and right the wrong he has done. Perhaps he was justified. I know he will blame her and will offer many reasons if I give him a chance. When a man wants, or does not want to do a thing, there is always an excuse. I don't think I'll be interested."

"Two wrongs never make a right. Don't do it boy." There was a pleading in his voice and tears in his eyes. "Laura is dead and nothing you can do will bring her back or undo what is done. No use to ruin your life and the lives of those who love him. After all, you're not God, and there's no use to play like you are."

"Just trying to help out a little. He won't mind me giving Him a nudge."

"Maybe the man was not to blame at all."

"He could have said 'No.' After all that has happened, I'm sure you will forgive me for saying this, but you're to blame more than either of them."

"Me?" He was stunned.

"You never should have married her," I continued. "You knew how much she wanted to be a mother, and you also knew you could not sire a child."

At the door I hesitated, turned and said, "A long, long time ago, I heard Laura say that a body has got to do what he has to do. She's dead now, and he killed her. I grant you he didn't put a gun to her head as I am going to do to his, but murder he did. And I intend for him to suffer for what he did to her and us!"

"Dead people do not suffer," the Cap'n said. "If he was a conscience, he has and will, suffer. Please don't do it, boy! It is too late to matter."

"It's never too late to even scores," I flung back at him as I opened the door and came face to face with Cindy.

"I heard you and the Cap'n talking," she said, as I closed the door softly and leaned against it. "I just had to eavesdrop. Perhaps I shouldn't have, but after all, you know, I have a stake in this affair," she told me bluntly.

"No, I didn't know," I answered.

"Oh, no?" There was a wide questioning look on her face. "Have you forgotten we were at one time all but married?"

"But that was before so much happened," I replied.

"As far as I'm concerned, it hasn't changed things a particle. I'm still in love with you. Does that make sense?" she inquired.

"No it doesn't; not under the circumstances."

"Just whose saddle blanket is the burr under?" she inquired, her voice rising to a high pitch. "Did the man rape the woman, or did the woman seduce the man? Has it ever occurred to you that you might have prevented all this by simply fathering the child?"

I looked at her a long time before replying. Horror must have been written on my face, because she refused to look at me. I spoke quickly, not pausing for breath, running my words together. "Now let me ask you something. The Cap'n has practically raised me from scratch. He spoon-fed me before I was old enough to know much about life. Why, I'd rather have my hands burned off at my wrists than to do anything that would make him unhappy! Of course I wanted to father her child. What young man wouldn't? But how can you stand there and say you love me, and yet think I would stoop so low?"

"Do you think the Cap'n is very happy with things as they are?" She took a step toward me and placed her hand on my arm. "I hope you would stoop so low as to seduce me here and now if it would deter you from doing what you are about to do. But no, you've got to play the part of young Lochinvar, stalking across yon cotton patch to shoot a dastardly coward who did not have enough willpower to say 'No' when your fair lady, sitting high and mighty on a pedestal you built with your own little hammer, asked him to get her with child."

The speech was too much for Cindy. She reached and grabbed a porch post, and her body shook with sobs. I did not go to her but still stood with my back to the door. "Had Henry Vaughn said 'No,' in time the Cap'n and Laura might have adopted children."

"Oh no, not Laura," she replied, drying her eyes. "She thrived on excitement; she had to feed her ego!"

"You are very unfair," I told her, shrugging wearily, wishing to get on with what I intended to do.

"You think I don't understand," she said, and came back to confront me again. "And I don't. I wish to God I did. It is hard to watch one you love go walking out of your life to kill somebody else's snakes."

"If you get a thorn in your thumb, you take your knife and cut it out. Maybe that's not a very good comparison, but I've got to do what I'm going to do."

Again she took hold of my arm and squeezed it as if she would force me to get her point of view. "It's easy to seduce a woman when she's getting what she wants. Laura wanted a baby. She got one. All that happened after she got what she wanted, might have happened even if the Cap'n had fathered Jody. What I can't possibly understand is why all the jumping at conclusions? And why is Henry Vaughn to blame for everything?"

"He could have said 'No.'"

"But he didn't, and neither would you under the same circumstances. So why all the fuss?"

"I just don't know." I drew my hand wearily across my face as if to brush aside something that blurred my vision. But to no avail. "It's all very confusing, and I can't seem to explain it to anybody's satisfaction but my own. Maybe I'm all mixed up. But of one thing I am sure. Before the snake came, we were very happy, and ever since, we've been very miserable."

"Will it relieve the misery for you to kill the snake?" she asked, shaking my arm violently.

"I just don't know. I'm afraid not. But that is what I'll never rest until I find out."

101

"Oh, fiddle," she said in disgust, seizing both my arms and shaking me like a dog shakes a rabbit, "might as well try to stack marbles as talk sense into your noggin. You are so like my father used to say about Collin's ram; 'You've got a head of your own, and you're determined to butt with it, even if you butt your brains out.' I'll save my breath to cool my soup. Go on have your fun. Shoot the rascal and see what happens. After it's all over, if they don't hang you, and you ever get out of the pen, I'll be waiting for you!" She reached up and kissed me and rushed into her room, her sobs echoing and re-echoing through the dogtrot.

I shivered deep inside myself and stalked out the front gate to start on a journey that lasted a little short of eternity.

# CHAPTER FOURTEEN

It is said that the leopard cannot change his spots, but when Frank James walked out through the dogtrot of the Big House on that far-off morning, he changed from the merciful to the unmerciful. He was a hunter, bound on a mission. He did not think of the consequences. His was a task he set himself to, and he would not turn back. He would lose his identity until such a time as this mission was accomplished. In so doing, he must go outside himself. He had not thought of becoming a murderer. Now he must become one. It would not be of his own volition, but of the inner man bound on vengeance. He would become a Dr. Jekyll and Mr. Hyde; two distinct personalities who operated within the same body.

The day was far spent when he opened the gate to Henry Vaughn's yard. He looked neither to the right nor left. He boldly walked upon the porch, threw open the front door, and saw the man he had come to destroy lying propped up with pillows on a bed; his face wan and pale; so pale it was difficult to tell where his features ended and the bedding began.

"I've come to kill you," Frank James said to the face on the pillow, his voice calm as if he were giving the time of day.

With but a flicker of his lids over the eyes that stared out of deep-seated sockets, the man on the bed said, "Had you waited another day or two, you could have saved your bullet and your energy." He turned his head wearily on the pillow, his face was that of one who had come to the edge of a precipice and dreaded to see what lay beyond. His eyes expressed nothing.

"Why do you say that?" The man at the foot of the bed had drawn his gun and now stood with it in his hand.

"I told you at my son's funeral that I was dying by inches. Now I've about run out of inches. In fact, the doctor told me just this morning that I am now working on the last few."

"Then it won't mean anything if I kill you?" The voice of the man with the gun sounded muffled and far away.

"Oh," said the voice from the bed, "it might satisfy your vanity or pride. You might feel like a knight in shining armor, going forth to seek revenge; to destroy a bastard who took advantage of a woman you had put on a pedestal, all because you learned the woman was only human and possessed feet of clay."

There was the smell of death in the room. Moments ran on. The only sound was the hurried breathing of the dying man and the ticking of a clock on a mantel over a fireplace.

The man on the bed noticed the one with the gun felt ill at ease. "Take a chair, won't you," he invited, "and let's talk things over."

Henry Vaughn was surprised when the man with the gun told him Laura was dead. They spoke of the day at the train, the death of the boy and his mother. They looked into the open graves. Together they gazed into the soul of a lonely woman who cried out against the pricks of fate that denied her motherhood. The gun lay on the bed forgotten, as the two cleared their throats, shifted their positions, and made small noises. They talked of little things forgotten, the night the dying man stayed for supper; of little things that mean nothing when they happened and heartbreaks when remembered.

Now he was walking, his steps slow and uncertain. He was not sure where he was headed. Should he return and report to the Cap'n what had happened in there in the house of misery Henry Vaughn had built? But he wasn't quite sure just what had taken place. He brushed a hand across his eyes and let it drop to his mouth, as he studied the landscape about him and tried to remember.

A veil of glimmering dust drifted up each time a vehicle passed. It settled over the roadside's underbrush of hedges, sassafras, sumac and persimmon, with their splashes of crimson and lemon-yellow colors. Beyond the bushes the woods were tossed in broken masses against the coming of night and the soughing of the wind in the lonely pines.

If he had only known; if he had looked ahead to all this the day he took Laura to the train to go away with the now dead-and-gone man! A dust like a gossamer veil enveloped him and did not go away. From out of the veil there came a voice. It asked if he would like a ride. He did not want to bothered. He wanted to be alone and try to remember. He did not reply, but a door was open, and like a sleep-walker, he entered and found a seat. He felt a weariness he had not been aware of, as if he had walked for many hours.

Where have you been?

Everywhere and nowhere; to the end of the earth and back to Bussey. But not today, not yesterday. It must have been a

105

long, long time ago. He was like a child repeating words he did not understand.

What did you do?

There was nothing wrong with the question. He wished he knew the answer, but he didn't. Soon, very soon, he was sure he would remember. Then he could tell the man beside him; the man who seemed so concerned. He had a bright star on his chest; a star not unlike those taking over the heavens where the God was that he set out to nudge. It was also like the ones yonder that became brighter as they came nearer.

When he got out of the car, he looked up. He didn't know why, just as he didn't know where he had been, where he was, or why he was where he was. Above him there was nothing and nothing and nothing, reaching away yonder like a hopeless shout; a crying out and a dying out of upper emptiness like the feeling inside him.

And far beyond, so many millions of times his own tallness that the number could not be counted, were the cold stars; little yellow lights of pain at the very top of the far distance and not unlike the ceiling of a room he had seen before he entered the car.

He was now in another room, a cold, dank room with a light in the center. He sat under that light on a stool which was not at all comfortable. He was very weary. His eyes smarted; his shoulders hunched as if he crouched to spring at the figures in the shadows just beyond the glow of the bright lights; figures with voices that did not cease.

There were questions and more questions; always questions and whys. They asked why did you do it and kept hoping they would change to ones he could answer. But they never did.

# CHAPTER FIFTEEN

The next thing he remembered, it was morning. A visitor came. When the steel door opened, and she came in, he was not sure he had ever seen her before. She must be someone who will ask more questions, he thought; so he decided to start with a question of his own.

"Why did you come here?"

"To ask you a question," the voice said.

He knew that. "But what question?"

"Why did you kill my husband?"

Now he knew who she was. Now he recognized her as the woman who interrupted his conversation with the dead man. She had bolted into the room, her eyes wide and questioning. Hate, such as he had never seen, burned deep within them. She was apparently in shock. She tried to speak, but nothing came out. She clasped and unclasped her hands. Her husband noted her agitation and asked what was wrong. For a moment she seemed to struggle for control, then blurted out, "It's time for your medicine. I'll get some water."

She returned with an empty pail. She was very calm, then. She said she would have to go to the well for fresh water. He volunteered to go instead. Yes, now he remembered, but not enough.

Now it all came back to him. For a tick of time he stood at the foot of the bed, saw a gun lying there in the bed's middle and, out of a haze, heard himself say, in answer to her last question: "Not necessarily. I realize he could have done it himself. I was very foolish to leave the gun where he could reach it, or where you could get to it for that matter."

"You had a good reason for what you did!"

"For what I did? I'm sorry, but I don't seem to follow you."

"I overheard your conversation. At times you were rather loud, you know."

"So you did use the gun?"

"You can believe that. In your trial you can even swear to it. Then I will swear to all you said to my husband. In that way you can drag the other woman's name through a lot of mud and slime."

"On the other hand, her name goes untarnished and I hang?"

"They won't hang you. He would have been dead in another day or two."

"Under those circumstances, why did you choose to hurry the matter?"

"I haven't said I did."

"Just why did you come here?"

"To give you a choice. I'm anxious to know what it will be."

"Does it really make much difference to you?"

Then, it was as if a curtain dropped quickly over the face of the woman at the bars. Her expression turned to one of fear and hatred. "Not a great deal," she finally said. "I rather think I'd like to behold her dirty linen hung on the line for all to see."

"She won't be at the trial."

"Why?"

"She's dead! Your husband killed her."

"So much the better."

"Your time is up, Mrs. Vaughn." The man with a star was at the bars.

As she turned, her mask came down, and suddenly she seemed very old, forlorn and broken. "I hope you'll do nothing you'll regret," she said over her shoulder.

That afternoon the Cap'n came to the jail with a lawyer. The prisoner was told he must put complete trust in this person who had been hired to help him.

"Nobody can help."

"Boy, you got yourself into a peck of trouble."

"I know."

"I guess for me to say I told you so wouldn't be a lot of help."

"Not exactly."

"Why did you do it?"

"Who said I did?"

"Everybody. They all say it."

"Everybody has been wrong before. In fact, when folks start jumping at conclusions, haven't you noticed they often jump the wrong way? And didn't you once tell Jody that 'They Say' was the biggest liar in the world"

"When you left, you said you was going to kill him."

"Couldn't I have changed my mind?"

"Why would you?"

"He was sick, wasn't he? He said he would be gone in a short time. I just couldn't do it on that account. I could see no point in kicking a dead horse."

"Would it help if you told us what really happened?" the lawyer asked.

"I'm not sure I know just what did happen. But I'll be glad to tell you what I think occurred, if you only promise me you won't pressure me into anything, and you both go along with what must be done."

The Cap'n, the lawyer and the prisoner, who was still called "Boy" by the Cap'n, talked in low tones for a long time; the one argued, the other two pleaded.

"If that's the case, we'll just tell the court and it will set you free," prompted the Cap'n.

"You'll tell the court exactly nothing," the prisoner emphatically retorted.

"But they may hang you, Boy."

"Well, so what? I've heard it said a person can get used to anything – even hanging. I'm not afraid of death. It's living that scares the daylights out of me."

"Now you're talking crazy, Boy."

"When you come right down to it, you both have to admit I'm right. The court wouldn't believe me. It's my word against a woman's, and you're both aware of what that means. I'm thinking about you, Cap'n, and Laura – even though she's dead."

"But not yourself?"

"That's right. Whatever it takes, I'm willing to go through with it. It's my funeral."

"We'll try to keep them from hanging you," interjected the lawyer.

"I wish you wouldn't."

"Do you think that's smart?" The Cap'n was decidedly puzzled. "Do you like the idea of being the goat? Does it give you some sort of morbid satisfaction?"

"No! To tell the truth it doesn't give me much comfort. I'm really scared to death. Maybe I'm like the boy passing a graveyard – just whistling to keep up my courage. But I've been everything else in this miserable affair. Why not the goat? Who cares?"

The Cap'n put his hand on the prisoner's shoulder and squeezed it so hard the Boy winced. "I care, Boy. I care very much. You'll never know how much. I'm enough concerned that I'm going to stay with you just as long as there's a red bean on the dish."

*OF WHAT WAS, NOTHING IS LEFT*

# CHAPTER SIXTEEN

The trial of *Frank James vs. The State of Arkansas* lasted seven long, agonizing days; days that stretched into years to the man whose life was weighed in the scales of justice. Spectators came from the three counties over which the Cap'n and the defendant had traveled as a buyer and hauler. Some came out of curiosity; some came with pity that showed clearly on their faces. Others were there to see a killer get his just desserts – whatever they were. The courtroom on the second floor of the old, crumbling and smelly building was packed. Not even a space to stand was left unoccupied.

The state paraded witness after witness to testify to the dead man's character. There was no question but what his actions were at all times above reproach. He was a loving husband, a kind neighbor and a gentleman, first, last and always.

Always except once, the defendant wanted to cry out. Time after time, he felt compelled to spring to his feet and tell them what he knew. But he remained silent. Let them think what they would. Wasn't it a quirk of the mind of man that he believed only what he wanted to believe? All dead men are not saints, he wanted to shout to the court. But he knew nobody would listen to one who had committed such a shocking crime.

When the wife of Henry Vaughn was called to the witness stand, a hush settled over the packed-in crowd. Here was the climax. Anything and everything she had to say would tend to tighten the noose around the neck of the one who so wantonly snuffed out the life of the man she loved. It mattered not to those who hung on the edge of their seats and listened to every word, that the man she loved so passionately would have been dead and buried this very moment; dead from a horrible disease. But that was something else again. There was no glamor, no suspense in such a demise.

"Do you swear to tell the truth, the whole truth, and nothing but the truth, so help you God?" – the court clerk intoned.

The faint flicker of a sardonic smile played around the corners of the defendant's mouth, as the witness answered in a scarcely audible tone, "I do." He watched anxiously as she had trouble with her hands. They fluttered to her face and back to her lap like birds when a hawk swoops overhead. She pushed back a stray wisp of hair that had escaped from under her hat. She would not tell the truth, of that the prisoner at the bar was sure. She was too much a woman to throw caution and pride to the wind and admit her mate had committed the act which made for so much despair and unhappiness among those whose lives he touched so briefly.

Someday this woman's testimony – word for word – the prisoner dared hope would come back to haunt the judge, the jury, and the eager, dead-quiet spectators.

The woman was asked by the prosecutor to tell her story. Many times she faltered. She kept her handkerchief before her face much of the time, so the man she had come to destroy could not look into her eyes. Now and then there was a long pause in her testimony while she sobbed. Many of the women in the crowded courtroom wept with her. They shared her troubles gladly because they were not theirs. Was she overcome with remorse, or did she try to impress the jury, the accused man wondered?

Her long story was finally finished, but the man who was anxious to further his political ambitions was not satisfied. He began plying her with questions; questions he was sure would spring the trap door to the gallows.

Q: You say you heard loud talk before you went into the room to see what was happening? Were you able to understand anything said?

A: I was not.

Q: Was this loud talk the first time you knew your husband had company?

A: Yes.

Q: You stated it was time for your husband's medicine. So you went into the room. You carried an empty bucket and told him you had to go to the well for fresh water?

A: That is correct.

Q: And the visitor – the defendant here – offered to go for the water?

Before she replied, the witness looked for a fleeting instant at the man she was trying to hang. The prisoner thought there was a glimmer of compassion therein; a plea for understanding. But the glance was so hurried, he might have misinterpreted it. She hesitated so long in her agitation, the lawyer repeated the question.

A: Yes.

Q: He then took the bucket and left the room? Is that correct?

A: That is correct.

Q: Did you stay with your husband until the man returned from the well?

A: No.

Q: What did you do?

A: I went to the kitchen to prepare the medicine.

Q: While you were in the room, did you see a gun either on the bed or on the defendant?

A: I did not. I had no idea why he had come.

Q: The next thing you heard was a shot?

A: Yes.

Q: You rushed into the room?

A: Yes.

Q: Where was the gun?

A: At the foot of the bed.

Q: Where was the defendant?

A: He stood at the foot of the bed.

Q: Where was the bucket of water he was supposed to have brought in?

A: I didn't notice; I was too disturbed. [This answer was but a whisper.]

Q: Did the defendant also appear to be disturbed?

A: Very much so.

Q: What was the condition of your husband?

Here the witness closed her eyes. A shudder passed through her body. Her sobs extended to the far reaches of the courtroom. The defense attorney rushed to her side and tried to soothe her with consoling words. The judge kindly admonished her to take her time to reply to the question.

A: The blood gushed from his forehead. He moaned and appeared to be dying.

Q: Did he say anything?

A: He asked, why did you do it?

Q: Was this inquiry addressed to the man at the foot of the bed?

A: Yes.

Q: Did the man at the foot of the bed attempt to reply?

A: He did not. He only shook his head from side to side and made no attempt to go to the aid of my husband.

Q: What happened next?

A: I asked him why he did it!

Q: What did he say?

A: He said he did not understand. He appeared to be in shock. He looked as if he would collapse.

Q: Was there a look of guilt on his face?

Def. Attorney: Objection, your Honor. That would be but an opinion of the witness.

Judge: Objection sustained.

Q: What did he say next?

A: Nothing. He just stood there for a long time. Finally he said, "I don't understand it. The man would have been dead in a week anyway." He then turned and walked out of the room and headed up the road. As soon as he left, I went to the telephone and called the sheriff.

Q: Mrs. Vaughn, do you have any idea why this man killed your husband?

Def. Attorney: Objection, your Honor. It has not yet been established that the defendant killed her husband.

Judge: Objection sustained. Her answer would be but a conjecture and not evidence in the case. The jury will ignore the question.

Dis. Attorney: That is all the questions I have, your Honor.

The defense counsel rose slowly to his feet. His face was clouded with anxiety. His steps toward the witness chair showed he felt defeat was inevitable. The spectators were tense. The witness stirred restlessly in her chair. She crossed and recrossed her legs.

Q: Mrs. Vaughn, a short time ago you swore to tell the truth, the whole truth, and nothing but the truth, so help you God. You realize, I'm sure, that your testimony may be such as to help destroy an innocent man. Do you, by any chance, wish to change any part of it?

The witness did not look up. The listeners held their breath. Finally, the witness shook her head slowly. A great sigh went up from the spectators; a sigh like the last breath of the dying.

The defense counsel turned quietly to the Judge. With despair in every line of his troubled face, he said, "That's all your Honor."

The sheriff gave his testimony in a loud voice, clear and arrogant. It was as if he felt he should be honored with a brass band and long speeches, all because he had tracked down and brought to justice – all by himself – a vicious killer.

"Maybe I'm all mixed up," the prisoner thought. But as he remembered it, nobody had tracked down anybody.

After the preliminaries were over, and the sheriff had fully convinced the listeners of his importance by his surly braggadocios, the prosecutor asked: "Did you find the gun the killer used while you were at the Vaughn home?

Def. Attorney: Your Honor, we have not as yet established who the killer was. Therefore, the witness cannot possibly know the answer to the question.

At this, the spectators looked at each other as if to ask, "We haven't?" The jurymen squirmed in their seats, their expressions plainly saying, "You think we haven't."

Judge: Prosecutor must change the wording of his question if he expects an answer.

Q: Did you find a gun on the premises?
A: You bet your sweet life I did.

Judge: The witness will answer the question and refrain from adding any of his feelings.

Q: Was the gun loaded?
A: With the exception of one bullet.

Q: Where was the gun?
A: On the bed.

Q: You were there shortly after the murder. Did the gun show signs of being fired recently?
A: It did.

119

Q: Were there any fingerprints on the gun?
A: Apparently, there was not.

At this answer, the man on trial for his life turned and looked directly at Mrs. Vaughn. She was fumbling in her purse and did not look up.

Q: What do you think happened to them?
Def. Attorney: Objections, your Honor. The opinion of the witness concerns the case in no way.

Judge: Objection sustained.

The questioning, the objections, the sustaining and overruling went on and on. The prisoner was very tired. He wished there was some way to prod the judge into pounding on the bench with his gavel and declaring the trial over and done with. Then he could get on with the sentence.

Q: You say you arrested the defendant near the scene of the murder?

Def. Attorney: Objection, your Honor. We have not yet established the fact that there has been a murder.

Prosecutor: We haven't? [The prosecutor seemed amazed at the statement.]

Def. Attorney: We certainly have not. If the gun was on the bed – as witnesses have testified – it could have been suicide.

Sheriff: Not on your tintype.

Judge: Mr. Sheriff, this court is not in the least interested in your opinion in this particular instance. If you speak out again without being asked, I shall be forced to fine you for contempt of court.

Q: Where did you arrest the defendant?

A: He was up the road a ways from the Vaughns.

Q: Did he offer any resistance?

A: No. He knew better than to put up a fight. [The Judge gave the sheriff a scathing look.]

Q: Did you question the defendant?

A: I did, several times.

Prosecutor: Will you tell the jury what you learned in this questioning?

The sheriff raised his right hand, used his thumb and index finger to form a zero, and said, "Exactly nothing."

The defense counsel hesitated to call the defendant to testify. He decided in the affirmative after he consulted the accused.

Once the defendant was in the witness chair, the lawyer was very careful in interrogating him. He established the fact that Frank James was at the Vaughn residence the day Henry Vaughn was shot. He did go for a bucket of water. He admitted there was a shot, but as to who did it, he was vague. He just didn't know. He admitted he was standing at the foot of the bed when Mrs. Vaughn came into the room.

He was sure the man on the bed had been shot. Yes, the gun was on the bed. He didn't know why he left it there. Yes, he went to the residence to shoot Henry Vaughn. No, he did not remember shooting him; he only knew he heard a shot and saw the man bleeding and heard him moaning. He did not know if the man was dead when he left the house, but he thought maybe it was.

Yes, he got in the car with the man they had been referring

to as the sheriff. No, the sheriff did not abuse him. He did ask about the shooting. He told the sheriff he did not know who did it.

The prosecutor hurried to his feet as soon as the counsel for the defense declared he was through with questions. He danced rapidly over to confront the witness. He pointed his finger at the accused and asked in a loud, angry voice, "Why did you do it?"

"Who said I did?"

The defense lawyer was on his feet to object.

The judge overruled the objection. "In every crime," the judge said, "there is a motive. We know there is one in this case, but we have not determined what it is. If the defendant will answer the question, that motive may be brought out and might have a decided bearing on the case."

The prosecutor continued to stare at the witness, who did not attempt to reply to this question. Again the lawyer demanded, "Why did you do it?"

Still there was no answer.

The judge raked the witness with hard eyes. "You are to answer the question," he demanded sternly.

"I'll answer his question when he answers mine," the witness said doggedly.

The audience began to buzz again. The judge rapped for order and threatened to clear the courtroom if it was not forthcoming. He again turned to the witness stand and said, "Mr. James, you are to answer the question."

"Maybe you would like to answer it, Judge, or maybe that fat bastard of a lawyer ought to answer it. If he can't, maybe that son-of-a-bitch who calls himself a sheriff can throw some light on the question. He seems to know everything else."

The witness sprang from the chair and stared at the judge, who was again pounding the bench for order. His face livid with rage, the defendant screamed at the judge, "What to hell difference does it make? You're going to hang me anyway! Why the hell don't you get it over with?"

The sheriff and two of his deputies rushed over and seized the defendant. They dragged him out of the room. The sheriff parted the packed and crowded mass of people in the aisle as a plowshare parts the sandy ground after a shower. The crowd stared in horror. The tempo of their talk rose above the continual pounding of the gavel and the shouting of the judge. "Order! Order!"

He's mad, they said. This has made him insane! He must have already been crazy to murder a good man, a sick man, the likes of Mr. Henry Vaughn! He has gone off his rocker for sure!"

*OF WHAT WAS, NOTHING IS LEFT*

# CHAPTER SEVENTEEN

It struck me as strange to look through the bars of my cell the next morning and see the sun come up. The trial was over. That was something to burn a candle and say a prayer about. Now I could go back to being me.

They had hustled me back to the courtroom after I calmed down from my outburst. I saw the strict face of the judge redden as I took my seat. Evidently, he was still disturbed over the scene I had made, but if he were honest with himself, he would have to admit that I completely scuttled the question which caused the furor.

In my absence, the defense lawyer had announced he was willing to get on with the arguments. It was just as well, for it was easy to see that our case was hopeless. The prosecutor was certainly in his element when bent on convincing a jury.

To hear him tell it, I had committed the crime of the century. He paced, he raved, he ranted. The listeners were led to believe there was no parallel in all the annals of law violation. I had murdered a man in cold blood; a man who had no blemish on his character, who had never lifted his hand to do any but charitable deeds. To turn me loose on society would be the same as releasing a mad dog on an unsuspecting community.

And why did I commit this dastardly crime? There was no motive given, and rightly so, for who could find a motive for the killing of an innocent man, unless he were the very incarnation of the Devil himself?

The defense lawyer, his brow furrowed formidably, paced slowly in front of the jury, his voice low and pleading. The prosecutor may have thought he was right when he said there was no motive, he told the twelve men. But he was wrong. There was a motive; a strong one. No, it wasn't brought out in the trial because the defendant was gentleman enough to take the consequences rather than do or say anything to add more hurt to lives already damaged beyond repair because of the murdered man.

The huddled audience buzzed once more. Spectators looked to the left and to the right. They wondered why they had been denied this juicy plum of gossip. Again the judge demanded order and again threatened to clear the courtroom.

The prosecuting attorney, with all his witnesses, the lawyer went on, has not proved my client committed murder. The law states clearly that there must be no doubt in your minds as to the guilt of the defendant. If there is even the least shadow of a doubt, you are to set my client free. His fate is in your hands. I hope you do no fail in your duty.

The jury was out for one hour by the courtroom clock. I failed to see why. Maybe they had trouble trying to decide whether to let me hang and get the misery over with, or send me up for life and prolong the agony. Anyway, to nobody's astonishment, they decided I was guilty and asked the court to show mercy, which was the same as telling the judge not to have me hung.

I looked at the judge and he ordered me to rise. His eyes were like blue coals of fire, and his voice was cold as breaking ice, as he said, "Frank James, you have been convicted of first degree murder by twelve of your peers. They have recommended that this court show mercy in sentencing you. That I am reluctant to do. You showed no mercy in snuffing out the life of a man whose name is above reproach. I am sorry I cannot sentence you to be hanged by the neck until dead. Do you have anything to say before I pronounce your sentence?"

"Yes, your Honor," the defendant replied. "I only wish to say that I hope you live to rue this day, because you are about to pronounce a sentence on an innocent man."

The judge was beside himself with anger. "Then," he said, and his voice was like thunder after summer lightning, "you think all the witnesses for the prosecution, the jury, and all the testimony were wrong?"

"I certainly do," came the reply.

"I would stake my life on their decision," he retorted with venom in his loud voice.

"Are you a good loser, Judge?"

He gave the accused a look intended to cower him into silence. Frank had had his say, but it fell on deaf ears.

"Tomorrow, Frank James," the judge said in as solemn voice as his temper would allow, "you are to be taken to the state penitentiary, where you are to spend the rest of your natural life, and may God have mercy on your soul!"

"Oh, my God! My God!" came from the Cap'n in a hoarse whisper that went running through the courtroom.

With a rap of the gavel, the judge declared the court

adjourned. He hurried out of the room, his black robe billowed around him. In my mind's eye, I could see Justice blindfolded, her unbalanced scales clasped in her hand. And I wondered if she was weeping behind the cover over her eyes.

The Cap'n and Cindy came early the next morning. The Cap'n wished we had put everything on the line and let the chips fall where they might have.

"Does it matter? Would they have believed it? Why not let the dead rest in peace?"

Cindy lingered after the Cap'n had said goodbye. She took one of my cold hands in both of hers and begged me not to give up hope. There would surely be a way! She promised to stay at the Big House and look after the Cap'n. She would write often. As she reached through the bars to kiss me good-bye, she again urged me to keep a stiff upper lip; but this was easier said than done.

# CHAPTER EIGHTEEN

Time has a habit of passing regardless of who does what.
Heartbreaks do not count with time. At Cummins Farm
the days were long and the walls were high. One finds little
time to think while he drags a cottonsack whose strap galls
the shoulders; shoulders stooped with grief at the loss of
freedom to come and go at will. The fear of another strap
at the sun's going down forced us all to give thought only to
getting our quota of cotton picked.

When the iron gates clang behind you, they take away
your pride, your hope and often your desire to live. I would
have gladly forfeited mine had it not been a longing akin
to pain to live long enough to see the day when I could go
home and say to the judge and those who condemned me,
"I told you so."

At night when the walls seem to move in and all but
smother you, there is nothing to feel. To many there is hope
because their sentences will eventually end. You will find
such inmates waiting, always waiting. But with lifers, there is
no tomorrow. The sameness was there yesterday; it is there
today; it will be there until the kind old nurse, Death, moves
in and takes over. Death is the sure cure for all diseases, the
end of all despair.

Cindy's letters came each week as she had promised. The
Cap'n seemed stronger than he had since the Pinto pony

had all but ended his sojourn here below. He faced up to the fact that three corners of the life's puzzle had been scattered like fall leaves before a harsh and biting winter storm. With Laura, Jody and me gone, he didn't have much will to live. Nothing he could do or say would restore even a semblance of these parts of the puzzle. He realized that so many of us live our lives out of season. In Indian Summer we blossom out, but then it is too late. The cold frosts of winter nip the bloom in the bud, and the too-late flower is doomed.

The Cap'n was now an old man, but he would not let the locust of time eat away the green of his spirit. He was never one to wallow in self-pity. Adversity, he knew, was part and parcel of every life. It wasn't always the burden that determined the final outcome, but the way it was carried, he reasoned. He had burdens enough, and some to spare, but he had seen others struggling along under greater loads. They had gone on; they had faced the sunshine and let the shadows fall behind them. He would go forth and do likewise.

The Percherons and the Maude mule were too old for further service and had been turned out to pasture. He didn't want this to happen to him. He bought a second-hand truck and again started to cover the three counties to buy up surplus animals, to make a living for Cindy and himself.

There is nothing in this life as permanent as change. The Cap'n soon learned that the buyer no longer made the price, and the seller had to take it or let it lie. The farmers now trucked their cattle into the county seat to market, where they were sold to the highest bidder in keen competition.

One night on his way home, discouraged and disillusioned from a day of frustrating attempts to buy what went for naught, the Cap'n lost control of his truck on the Dorcheat

Bridge. They found him pinned beneath the wreck, where he must have been most of the night.

His life, rather than his death, Cindy wrote, was almost more than she could bear. He had tried unsuccessfully to carry on after his world had been rent asunder. It would have been better, much better, she was sure, had he died the day he was thrown from the Pinto pony. He would have been spared so much futile living.

The tragedy of longevity, she said, is that all the other guests leave the party first. The one left is there among the ashes, dirty dishes and left-over food, crying "Wait for me!" in the empty room.

What is my cross, I thought, my wretchedness, my misery when compared to what his had been? As I looked back at all the seemingly mere trifles of the experiences, I wondered which was the most important in bringing us all to the place where we were. Thoughts of the death of the three I had loved and lost drifted like straws on the surface of my mind and left me with a profound and incurable melancholy.

I was sick and could not attend the Cap'n's funeral. Some-how it was a relief to have an excuse not to go. It was easier, much easier to remember him as he was at the trial, urging me to save myself because it was not I who had brought all this travail to pass.

He had willed the Big House and its surrounding acres jointly to Cindy and me. So he must have intended for us to marry. But what woman in her right mind would want a criminal for a husband? And, besides, I was to be incar-cerated for the length of my natural life. The judge had said so. What profiteth a man if he has half an interest in a farm and no freedom to go with it? The man must have had something in mind to give me a share of all his worldly

goods with the cousin of the woman he had loved so unwise-
ly. I felt a gratitude I could not put my tongue to. But what
difference did it make? It was too late to tell the donor.

Cindy came to visit me after she buried the Cap'n and
boarded up the Big House. She wanted to marry me there
in prison, but I wouldn't hear to it. How could we walk in
the sunshine when the shadow of the prison stretched so far?
She argued we had lost, but we still had each other, and that
was what counted.

There were tremors lying in waiting in her voice as she
said, "The land will not go away and neither will I. If you
are ever set free – and you will be – we both will be there
waiting."

She returned to Shreveport. I went back to my cell, more
depressed than ever. In the bleak dawn of reason, any dream
I had of ever leaving prison withered like flowers blighted by
a frost. I had asked little of life. I did not ask for cake, only
for bread. And what had I received?

I might as well have not asked. The Cap'n, Laura and Jody
– were they alive – would have said the same. And Henry
Vaughn and his wife! Perhaps the murdered man thought
when he was in Laura's arms he was partaking of life's
choicest morsels. But, in the end, it had soured in his mouth.
The passion that had ruined his life, the life of his only child
and his paramour, had also ruined mine.

All the things that I had tried to forget; things I had only
dimly perceived when they happened; impulses, unacknowl-
edged desires were flitting impressions like the shadow of a
summer cloud as it passes over the sun. Then, as suddenly
as they came, the visions flickered out. There I was, huddled
in my cell where the nights were longer than the days, and
hope was a will-o'-wisp I had no strength or will to pursue.

One day, after five years of my stay at Cummins Farm, the warden sent for me. Word had come that I was to be set free. Henry Vaughn's wife had died. Before her passing, she had admitted that she killed her husband in a fit of temper on that far-off day, centuries ago.

I took the cheap, ill-fitting suit and the tiny sum of money the state gives to all discharged prisoners. I almost ran to the station to catch the train. As it rumbled toward Jubilee, every click of the wheels on the rails seemed to be saying, "Free! You're free! At last, you're free!"

I walked the eight miles from the station to the Big House. Something told me if I were to find any part of what I had lost, it would be there.

And my hunch was right. Cindy, too, had the same feeling. It was in the dusk of evening. The sun had disappeared in a burst of wild colors beyond the pines west of the Big House. Suddenly, in the fading twilight, a ghostly figure came running up the road past the burying ground. I did not need anybody there to tell me who it was.

"How did you know?" I asked, after we had clung together for a thousand heartbeats.

"Good news sometimes travels fast, too. Besides, how does the swallow know when spring has come?"

And that was answer enough.

# THE END

*OF WHAT WAS, NOTHING IS LEFT*

# AFTERWORD

I now know that while my grandfather was a man with multiple interests, his passion was writing; crafting stories and narratives in poetic fashion. He probably did all those other things so he could indulge his creative muse. As a songwriter, I now "get it" in a way I never did when I was younger. Thanks to him, I like to believe.

*Of What Was, Nothing Is Left* certainly inspired me, and it made me think, too. After all, in addition to telling a story, it also reflects the reality of the time it represents. That is to say, some of the attitudes regarding race and other social issues are certainly out-of-step from how we as a society think today. But the context of the time matters, which is why I decided not to remove some of the references. This story was written a long time ago, and I'm not in the business of re-writing history.

I knew Fred Starr until he died in 1973. He was the very first person I'd ever actually personally known to pass away. I still feel the sting of that rainy night when I was told of his passing. But now I feel I truly know him through the beautiful work he left behind. And I am grateful. Do I wish he was still here to listen to what we have been working on? Of course. Do I think I would still be learning from him? Absolutely. I've started suggesting more and more to folks I know, if your grandparents are still here, sit with them and record their stories. Document your family history. And don't be afraid to ask the hard questions. This is how we protect and preserve history. This is how we help our loved ones live on.

*David Starr*